Saving Sophia

FLEUR HITCHCOCK

For Ian

- - - - - - - - -

First published in the UK in 2014 by Nosy Crow Ltd
The Crow's Nest, 10a Lant Street
London, SE1 1QR, UK

Nosy Crow and associated logos are trademarks and/or registered
trademarks of Nosy Crow Ltd

Text © Fleur Hitchcock, 2014
Cover illustration © Jim Field, 2014

The right of Fleur Hitchcock to be identified as the author of this work
has been asserted by her in accordance with the Copyright, Designs
and Patents Act, 1988

A CIP catalogue record for this book is available from the British Library

Printed and bound in the UK by Clays Ltd, St Ives Plc
Typeset by Tiger Media Ltd, Bishops Stortford, Hertfordshire

Papers used by Nosy Crow are made from wood grown in
sustainable forests.

ISBN: 978 0 85763 174 9

www.nosycrow.com

Life with the
stick insects

"Lottie," says Ned, thundering uninvited into my bedroom. "Will they let me take Oddjob to Bream?"

I stare at the thing in his hand. It used to be a stick insect, it might still be a stick insect, but mostly, it just looks like a stick.

"Not now, Ned, I'm busy," I say. "Actually, could you get out of my room?"

He's still standing there. I can feel it, but I go back to the tricky business of hiding my makeup deep inside my bag and try to ignore him. It's Dad's old rucksack and I'm packing it to take with me to

Bream Lodge Active Pursuit Centre.

I don't want to go.

I really don't want to go. But Ned wants to go so I have to go – because we always do everything together, whether or not I want to, and anyway Mum and Dad want to go moth-hunting in Cornwall – WITHOUT US.

Not that I want to go moth-hunting.

I stuff two old paperbacks down the side of the bag. *The Mystery of the Severed Foot*, and *One Against Many*.

"Ned, go away – I didn't ask you in."

"Why are you stealing Mum's books?"

"Ned, GO AWAY!"

He charges out, slamming my bedroom door behind him and the lump of plaster shaped like the Isle of Wight that's been clinging to the ceiling finally gives up the struggle against gravity, and crashes to the floor.

"Soreeeeeeee," he says, sticking his head back around the door. "Actually, she – Mum – wants you." And he slams the door again.

"Why?" I say, picking my way through a cloud of plaster dust.

Ned's already halfway up the stepladder to the

loft. It replaces the stairs that fell down last August when Dad tried to fix them. "Dunno," he says. "She's not cross with you or anything." He vanishes into the darkness.

Letting the rucksack slide to the ground, I creep out on to the landing. I don't want to pack because I don't want to go to stupid Bream Lodge, which is as utterly dull as this place; absolutely nothing happens here, absolutely nothing happens there. Perhaps if I haven't packed, I won't have to go and I can be bored in my own bed, or not bored, because in my bed I can read, and when I read, I can escape.

For a wonderful moment I let myself into the world of stories. It's a place where things happen and interesting people live. I go there every night. I read and I dream, and I'm happy because it's full of colour and excitement.

Behind me, a final small piece of plaster slips from the ceiling and plummets to the floor.

My life is not just dull, it's skanky, too.

Mum, Dad and another woman's voice float up from the kitchen below. It *sounds* like Miss Sackbutt from school but it can't possibly be. I've kept this house a closely guarded secret for the whole year that I've been in her class and I've let no one, absolutely no one, in or anywhere near the place. There is no way that I want anyone to know anything about our house; if they knew how grim it was, I'd never live it down.

I stand and listen at the top of the stairs.

It's all because of my parents. They're not normal; they're scientists. For fun, they read pamphlets about soil composition. Visit the compost heap. Or, for a treat, they take us to the National Humus Society headquarters in Okehampton where we eat alfalfa sprout sandwiches.

Sunday lunch is road kill.

I bet no one else has parents like mine.

I think of the last parents' evening – Dad smelled of silage, Mum wore a boiler suit – and I shudder.

I wish they could be like other people – wear suits, work in offices, eat ready meals. Watch telly. Then I could have friends home.

I could have friends. Full stop.

I approach the staircase. I'm going as quietly as I can, but the steps are tricky; the third tread's missing and the rest creak like coffins. When I reach the bottom, I lurk in the dark shadow under the stairs so that I can see into the kitchen.

There's a man. A stranger. He's tall and wearing

a very expensive suit. I know it's an expensive suit because Sarah-Jane Parkins' dad wears one like it so it must be. His face is turned away from me but I can see there's a twitch in his smoothly shaven jaw. Everything about him is perfectly turned out. Like a really smart bouncer.

I stare hard through the gap, collecting every clue I can from his appearance.

He's spotless, and despite looking like he's auditioning for the next James Bond movie, there's something altogether piggily pink about him, something that reminds me of a sausage, or a pork chop. It's probably the short blonde bristles sticking out over his collar.

Behind him bobs a minty green dress, stretched tight over a round shape. It *is* Miss Sackbutt and she's talking. "So when Mr Pinehead asked if he could meet someone else who was going on the school trip to Bream Lodge, I thought of Lottie, she's such a sensible girl, just the sort of influence Sophia needs, and I'm so sorry, I should have rung, but there's so little time, and he very sweetly offered to give me a lift in his rather wonderful car, and I still need to pack, seeing as we're off tomorrow…"

Her voice tails off. I wonder if she's caught

sight of the South American fungi that Dad's been cultivating on top of the fridge.

Wonderful car? *Definitely* a spy.

"Of course, of course." That's Dad's voice. "Bream, excellent spot — home of the first Earl of Bream of course, he of the breadplants, eighteenth century castle, built in the baronial style—"

"Bob, shhhh," says Mum. "They want to know about the outward-bound place." She addresses the man. "It's not very smart, you know."

"We don't need smart — just safe," he says. He's got a soft voice that doesn't go with the twitchy jaw. "Somewhere to keep Sophia tucked up and cosy while we get on with one or two things. Good idea of yours, Miss Sackbutt, keeping the children busy over the holidays."

"Oh — thank you, yes," says Miss Sackbutt. She lets out a silly high-pitched laugh. The same one she does when the vicar comes to school. She fancies him, too. "It does prove helpful to some parents."

"It's supposed to be educational as well," says Mum, grinding eggshells in a pestle and mortar with such force that she has to shout over the noise.

"Naturally, educational too," says the man, "but

it's very handy, and — like here — a long way from London. Almost remote."

Mum looks at him over her pestle and mortar. "So," she says. "What brings you here, Mr Pinehead? To our 'remote' patch of England?"

"Business," he replies. He pulls at his cufflinks. They're gold, they catch the light.

"Oh, how interesting — what kind of business?" asks Miss Sackbutt.

"Yes, what exactly?" says Mum, pausing in the demolition of the eggshells.

There's a long silence. I wait for him to say MI5. Instead he says, "A bit of property development."

"Gosh — how thrilling!" giggles Miss Sackbutt. "Do tell, where?"

"Place called the Grange?" he says. "It's up a tiny lane…" His voice tails off and I hear Mum's sharp intake of breath.

"Goodness — anyway," she says, too loudly. "I wouldn't really call Bream *cosy*. More like *shabby*. Your daughter might find it a bit basic."

Miss Sackbutt raises her eyebrows. "Shabby? Oh, I wouldn't say that. It's just back to nature; there are no frills, if that's what you mean. Anyway, I thought it would be good if the girls met before we left."

"LOTTIE!" yells Mum. I can tell that the pink man mentioning the Grange has irritated her.

Miss Sackbutt sidesteps suddenly, as if she's avoiding something on the floor. Mum's got a broom out and she's making the noises of someone who wants to drive people away: fierce sweeping and cupboard doors slamming. Then she says, "Do excuse me, Miss Sackbutt, Mr Pinehead. I just need to see to the chickens."

A cold draught on my face, a clunk, and Mum goes out of the back door. She slams it so hard that it bounces back open and swings wide, letting all the cold damp of the outside join the warm damp of the inside.

"Of course they should meet – LOTTIE!" bellows Dad.

I'll have to go in now.

The glazed
eye

Apart from Miss Sackbutt and the man, there's a girl I couldn't see before: a slight, perfect girl probably my age. She looks absolutely nothing like the man, who has his hand resting on her shoulder. He's too blond with sharp pale eyes, while she's dark, her skin a delicious dark brown, her eyes practically black. She has a long plait threaded with gold running down her back. If she told me she was an Indian princess, I'd believe her.

She's staring at the floor.

I blush. The floor's filthy, even filthier than normal. Dad's been taking plant cuttings on the kitchen table all day. There are five hundred tiny pots lined up and waiting to go into the green house, each with its own twig. Then I realise she's staring at my shoes. Mum's old red-leather walking boots; I've been trying them on for size.

I blush again.

"Charlotte, meet Sophia; Sophia, Lottie," says Miss Sackbutt, a particularly idiotic smile spreading across her face. "Lottie's such a sensible girl, and she's a big fan of detective novels, aren't you, Lottie? Whodunnits, *Cluedo*, you know the kind. 'Murder in the library' and all that. Do you like that sort of thing, Sophia?"

A look of incomprehension crosses Sophia's face and I glare at Miss Sackbutt. She's made me sound like a frump and anyway she's got it all wrong – I'm not sensible, I am never sensible. And I don't like whodunnits, I like challenges: heroes facing the impossible, life and death situations, people clinging to the sides of mountains by their fingertips. Sophia looks up at me for an explanation.

"It's only because there's nothing else to do round here…" It sounds lame, and I realise that the best thing would be to keep my mouth shut but instead I keep talking.

"So I really like reading, especially adventure fiction. It's really exciting…"

Stupid. Stupid. Stupid.

The kitchen falls silent, as if everyone's run out of things to say. The blond man clears his throat and checks his phone. Miss Sackbutt coughs, and I hear Mum down by the chicken sheds, clanking bin lids and slamming gates. Dad rootles in a cupboard, searching for something.

A slug makes its way out of the kitchen door.

"What kind of thing do you read, Sophia?" I ask, my mouth forming the words of its own accord.

Sophia shrugs. I give myself an imaginary kick and vow not to say another word.

"So." Miss Sackbutt must find the silence as agonising as I do because she touches the man on the sleeve and giggles. "Oh dear, yes, the Grange, my, what a place." She stops.

The man looks at her as if he'd like to brush her hand away, but smiles instead. He doesn't use his eyes, but his mouth stretches wide.

"I didn't realise the Grange was even on the market," says Dad, reaching into a cupboard.

"It wasn't, isn't," the man says, smoothly. "We inherited it, unexpectedly. Now I'm toying with how best to deal with it. Looking at the potential – turning it into a country-house hotel, golf, spa, you know the sort of thing."

"I didn't teach you, did I, Mr Pinehead?" asks Miss Sackbutt suddenly, peering into one of Mum's glass tanks. "So many people have been through my hands." About half a centimetre from the end of her nose a scorpion stops what it's doing and peers back.

The man rubs his hair. It's short, and I suspect that there's less of it than he'd like. "Er – no. I'm not local – I've never been down here before, in fact. And what a lovely, unsophisticated part of the world it is. Anyway, the old lady that owned the Grange, she was a, er, distant relative."

"Goodness – lucky you," says Dad, not really listening. "Right," he adds, slamming a plastic bottle on to the table and unscrewing the lid with his teeth. "New friends going to Bream Lodge, that calls for a celebration, don't you think, Lottie? This year's gooseberry champagne – who'd like to try a little?" He waves the bottle at Miss Sackbutt and grabs four smeary glasses from the draining board.

Miss Sackbutt wears spectacles that make her

look like an owl and she can do this thing with her eyes to make them perfectly round. She does this now and gazes owlishly at the thick yellow liquid, before resting her lip doubtfully on the edge of the cloudy glass. About now, she'll get the smell of the gooseberries, slightly fermented and sour. I watch to see if she'll go ahead and drink it.

It looks exactly like a cup of fresh horse wee.

The man's got one, too. His eyebrows have gone up into his hairline. I don't suppose this is his usual kind of drink, and I watch Sophia watching him. She's got a smile on her face. She catches my eye before staring down at the floor again.

Dad picks up his glass and knocks the liquid back, then slams it on to the table before refilling it. "Nectar," he declares. "Strained through Cleo's winter tights to remove the yeast mothers and mixed with my secret ingredient."

Oh no.

"What's the secret ingredient?" asks Miss Sackbutt, her mouth shrinking to a tiny circle and her eyebrows lifting above the rims of her spectacles.

Dad leans to whisper in her ear and Miss Sackbutt's mouth drops open; the glass, rescued by

Dad, makes it back to the table, and the man puts his by the sink. Untouched.

Dad starts talking about Bream Lodge, and I catch Sophia's eye again; this time she risks a proper smile and I smile back.

Like a shadow, Ned appears at my elbow with a bag of Mum's homemade parsnip and beetroot crisps. He offers them to Sophia. She takes a microscopic shard of beetroot crisp and slips it in between her teeth.

"Good, aren't they?" says Ned, and she nods, presumably because she can't speak. I grab a parsnip crisp and grind it with my molars. It's horrible. Not only is it thick and chewy, but it's stale. I sigh. Just as it looks like someone interesting's going to Bream, she has to come to the house first. She'll never be my friend now. Ever.

I watch as she takes the beetroot crisp out of her mouth and slips it into one of Dad's flowerpots.

I can't blame her.

The man's talking. "Sophia's between schools at the moment and I need a few business days – a quick trip to New York, tedious visits to the planners, bank manager, lots of dull stuff. Property development's new to me, so it all takes longer than

it ought. That's why I took advantage of the Bream Lodge trip, and there was a spare place, and Sophia seemed happy to go..."

He's not a regular property developer? I revert to my earlier analysis. So he could still be a spy. Or a butcher who goes to New York? A meatball specialist, perhaps. Or is it industrial espionage? He's off to spy on American fast-food companies. I look at him again. I can just see him sneaking past vats of boiling meat with a micro camera in his hand.

Sophia glides across the kitchen, eyeing the tanks of scorpions. She's pretending to study her nails which, perfectly filed, lie at the end of her delicate fingers. She's utterly beautiful.

I blush again, because I'm not. I'm an apple-shaped thing; red-cheeked with hazel eyes, coarse mousey-brown hair and crooked teeth. My clothes don't fit and I'm aware that, unlike Sophia's, my stomach curls over the top of my trousers.

We might as well come from different planets, but I think I want Sophia as my friend. Quite badly.

Ned empties the few crisps he hasn't eaten into a pudding basin and Mum bursts through the kitchen door, speckled with goosegrass seeds. She's holding a dead chicken upside down by its back legs.

"Supper," she cries, thwacking it down on the table. "When I've plucked and drawn it." She gazes round the room, challenging anyone to say anything.

The chicken's glazed eye stares up at the lampshade.

I can't even look.

I simply want to die.

Burnt

orchids

"I cannot believe that beautiful place is now owned by that awful man!" yells Mum, slamming forks back into the cutlery drawer. "'A golf course', he says! We'll have to start a campaign to Save the Grange – signatures, letters to the papers, lobby the Department of the Environment."

"Will we?" asks Dad. He's watering his cuttings with a pipette, five drops each.

"You know we will – it's the most wonderful site, completely untouched since the '20s, and the barn's full of horseshoe bats." Mum jams the drawer and yanks it backwards and forwards until a chip of

17

wood pings into the room. "And I'm sure there were burnt orchids there last time I went. Then there's the walled garden, and that orchard stuffed with mistletoe – the last cider orchard in the village. It's just…magnificent. The whole thing's tragic."

"Ah," says Dad.

"Oh, *honestly*," says Mum, and she stomps back out into the almost completely dark garden.

"Oh dear," says Dad, shaking his head.

I look at him. "What is the Grange?"

Dad sighs. "Last known nesting spot of the Devon corncrake, and awash with nightingales in June—"

"Yes, yes," I interrupt. "Is it where Irene used to live?"

Dad straightens and wipes a speck from his glasses. "Yes. And of course Irene was a bit of a hero in your mum's eyes. I don't know what's upsetting her more, the fact that it was Irene's home or the scientific interest of the place."

I think about the house. I never knew it was called the Grange; it was always just "Irene's house" to me. I'm sure the grounds are special, the orchards are pretty, but they're only trees after all – it's the Irene part that worries me. "What about the actual

stuff inside? Will he have inherited that, too?"

"I expect so," says Dad, inspecting the pipette. "Usually the whole lot goes to the relatives."

I remember the sitting room. Sunlight over the wooden floor, tatty Persian rugs, the smell of wood smoke, an aeroplane propeller. Irene's mohair rug folded over her lumpy old legs. And the bookcases: rows and rows of old paperbacks, adventure stories, mysteries, romances, hours and hours of reading. I think of the man in the expensive suit slinging them into a heap and an unexpected tear springs to my eye.

"But, Dad — that's not right — I mean, he didn't even know her. Who keeps her memories?"

"How do you mean?"

"Once the house is gone, and the stuff's gone, what's left of Irene?"

Dad shrugs. "Her deeds, I suppose. The amazing things she did. Sadly, Lottie, the rest's not really up to us."

Upstairs, Ned flushes the toilet and a sound like an ocean liner starting its engine reverberates through the house.

"What will he do with it all?"

"If he hasn't already, he'll probably sell the things

that are worth anything in an auction and give the rest of it to house clearers. I'm afraid, in the end, most people just use a skip to clear out the things they can't sell."

"That's terrible," I say. "No wonder Mum's upset." I imagine the man going through Irene's personal things, her dressing table dotted with perfume bottles, the cupboard of old wooden toys, and throwing things into a bin bag. "She had a lovely Noah's Ark, I used to play with it, half the animals had legs missing – I couldn't bear him chucking that out."

Dad sighs. "It's hard, but it's the way of the world, love. Perhaps Irene wasn't thinking very clearly when she left it to him. Though we *have* only met him for a minute – he might be very sensitive underneath."

"He doesn't look sensitive. He looks more like a bouncer."

"But they're only things, love. It's the woman herself that's important." He gazes out of the window as if she was standing in the garden. "Irene Challis was a wonderful woman. She flew spitfire aeroplanes in the war, you know, taking them from the factories and delivering them to the airfields."

He smiles at me, and peers into a pot of earth. "She didn't have radio and had to fly blind into the fog." He stops to stare into the distance. "She crash-landed in Scotland once in one of those fogs."

"In *Calm Before the Storm*, Richard Standfast lands a plane in the desert in a sandstorm," I say.

Dad looks at me over his glasses. "Yes, Lottie, but deserts don't have stone walls and sheep and bothies. Irene got clear of the wreckage and walked miles on her own across Scotland in gale-force winds with nothing but an aviator's map to guide her. So far as I know she had nothing to eat. Took her a week.

"Anyway, she was a bit of a looker, by all reports. She was married and widowed twice during the war, and after the war, she married again, this time to a surgeon, but she never had any children." Dad refills his pipette from a jug of clear liquid. "Instead, she trained as a doctor, and then as an eye surgeon. She worked as a volunteer for the Red Cross in war zones in her holidays. By the time your mother knew her, she'd retired, her husband had died and she was fundraising for the Red Cross, growing vegetables and reading those detective novels with a magnifying glass. By the end, she was almost completely blind."

"I never realised that," I say. "Though I remember her feeling the animals from the Ark before telling me which ones were which. She had big lumpy hands."

"Arthritis," says Dad.

"And very thick glasses," says Ned, bursting into the kitchen. "She had newts in her pond, and played old records on an old record player."

"She always gave us custard creams and grape juice," I say.

"She played crazy golf with us in the garden," says Ned. "With a cup and a ping pong ball."

"She wore shorts and had veiny legs. And she laughed a lot."

"Yes, and she sang beautifully, and played the piano until she died." Dad loads up a tray of cuttings. "I think you'd describe her voice as a rich contralto. Anyway, your mum was devoted to her; she wouldn't want to see her house ruined." He pushes out through the back door. "If it was redeveloped, it would break her heart."

"Yes, it would," says Mum, crashing in through the door again, swinging the plucked chicken

behind her. "I couldn't bear to see more men like that one rolling up in their BMWs and swinging their golf clubs over what used to be Irene's lawn. I'd... I'd cry."

"I bet they'd build a swimming pool in the walled garden," says Ned. "And put lights all over the place which would confuse the glow-worms so they'd all die."

I watch Mum hacking the chicken into squares and throwing them into a casserole pot. She sniffs loudly.

"Couldn't we rescue all the stuff that's hers?" I say. "All the books?"

Mum lays down the cleaver and goes over to run her bloodied hands under the tap. "They're not ours, Lottie, so strictly speaking that would be stealing. But it all seems very odd to me. I thought Irene had left everything to a great niece. I've been waiting to hear from the solicitors about it." Mum glances at the Welsh dresser. "I've got a key. Somewhere. And I've already borrowed a few books but unless that man has a penchant for adventure fiction, I don't think he'll miss them. Maybe it wouldn't hurt to rescue one or two other things."

"Well, then it would be all right, wouldn't it?" I

say. "Because other than that it's only a house, and the last time I saw it, it had little trees growing out of the gutters and moss all over the stone — it needs doing up, it could be lovely if it was a spa…" I stop. Mum's eyes have filled with tears, and I feel out of my depth.

She turns towards me. "It's not that it doesn't need doing up, Lottie — it would be lovely to see it restored to its former glory. But there's a difference between wrenching up trees and putting in golf bunkers, and simply mowing the grass." Mum wipes her nose on her sleeve. "And a hotel is a very different thing to a home; I just can't bear to think of it all ripped out and replaced with fakery, it would be—"

"I understand," I say quietly. Although I don't, not entirely. Apart from anything else, I don't know how I feel about it. I don't want the man in the expensive suit to have Irene's things; I don't really want him bossing builders about, standing by Irene's old iron bedstead, his shined shoes on her worn rag-rug, but I also love the idea of what the house could become, the skanky kitchen gone, the rooms all white and gleaming. The steps cleared and fixed. The trees cut back away from the front

of the house.

I open my mouth to speak again, and decide not to.

Perhaps I'll ask Sophia about it while we're away; she must know something.

If she'll want to be seen with me.

Only friends
lie for you...

The coach leaves in ten minutes. Dad's offered to drive us to school but I wish he hadn't. Our car was built in the last century – the last millennium, even. It used to be red, but the red's gone and now it's kind of silver, except at the bottom where it's still red. Last time Mum took it to a car wash half the paint came off.

I hate it.

On the way here, we passed Irene's house, shaded by the tall ash trees that now surround it. A squirrel threw itself along the branches as we drove past, and the windows looked back at us blank and dark.

It made me feel deeply sad.

And cross.

We park next to a huge black Range Rover that is so big our car could probably park inside it. At the back stands Sophia, looking tiny, by a pile of green and gold luggage that includes a tennis racket and a violin. They seem ambitious for Bream that, as I remember it, is mostly mud or sand. She doesn't look very happy.

I try to think of something to say. *Hi — remember me? The one who talks too much?* Or *Sorry about Mum and the dead chicken.* Or *I'm beautiful inside, I'm just trapped in blubber.*

I don't say any of it.

Dad springs out of our car and I realise he's wearing a boiler suit and orange wellingtons and is in need of containing in case he attempts any social interaction. I struggle out past Ned's walking poles and grab Dad, pushing him back towards the car before he has a chance to mingle.

"Can you get my bag out, please, it's really heavy?" I ask as Ned nudges past and plunges into the boot of the car through the back seat before dragging his bag over my foot.

"Ow! Ned!" I squeal, but he ignores me.

"Are you wearing make-up, sis?" he asks. "Miss Sackbutt won't like that — how'd you sneak it past Mum?"

"Shhh! Ned, shut up or I'll use Oddjob as a hairclip."

"Oh, I didn't bring him in the end; brought Pinky and Perky instead. Thought Roman snails would be less trouble. Oh, and Dad, thanks for lending me the compass watch," he says, tightening the laces on his walking boots. "So looking forward to orienteering on the moor. I've already signed up."

"Excellent stuff," says Dad, pulling out my backpack and wincing at the weight. "Shame you couldn't have the smaller one, Lottie, but if Mum and I go to Cornwall for a couple of days moth-hunting, then we'll need it. You'll mostly be flopping about in the mud at Bream, I should imagine; just leave this old thing in the bunkhouse."

I kick my ridiculous rucksack. It looks like something the Victorian army might have used on manoeuvres. I glance around; everyone else has something small and pretty with logos and nylon iPod holders. I could cry.

Dad gives it an affectionate stroke. "Took me to the Hindu Kush, this rucksack. Probably still got

Afghan mountain sand in the pockets." He slaps it to demonstrate and a cloud of dust covers several nearby parents. "Sorry," he says, and gives me a peck on the cheek. "Shall I get out of here – would that be a good idea, pet?"

I nod, blinking back the tears.

"Oh – and just in case – I know you're not supposed to take any money, but here's some change." He drops a fifty pence coin into my hand. "You never know."

"Bye, Dad," says Ned.

"Bye, both. Have a good time, don't be a bother to Miss S." Dad leaps back into the car, slamming the door and leaving a flake of red paint on the tarmac.

I watch the car disappear down the road. Ned goes to join his friends, Tom and Ollie. They're comparing penknives and sleeping bags.

I kick the rucksack once more, and sit on it. I'm probably crushing my illicit packets of real factory-made crisps, but I don't honestly care; I'd like to stick the stupid thing through a shredder and I'd run away if it wasn't that the whole world must be staring at me, all the parents in their proper suits, mothers in skirts with tights and high heels, fathers with ties.

And all the other children.

I sneak a look around. Sophia's dad's talking to Mrs Parkin. She's fluttering her eyelashes at him. He's leaning on a gatepost, his long legs loosely crossed at the ankle. I can't work out what I think about him. He's smart, he's smooth, he's probably really clever, but somehow, I don't trust him.

He seems like he belongs on another planet.

He's probably spying on the Parkins; they're probably part of the international sausage-meat trade. Except I think that Sarah-Jane's dad is actually a neurosurgeon. Whatever they all are, they've got far more money and far more style than we have.

I turn the fifty pence over in my hand. Fifty pence? What can you buy with that? When did Dad last go to the shops?

I gaze at a ladybird scurrying over the tarmac. It skirts Ollie's trainer and hides in a crack by a bollard.

"That your dad, Charlotte?" asks Sarah-Jane Parkin, from behind me.

I nod, fighting back the tears but they sneak past my eyelids.

"Oh," she says. "Does he always wear those wellingtons?"

I don't answer. Sarah-Jane is probably the last person I'd choose to go on any kind of holiday with; it's really better to watch ladybirds crossing the tarmac than make conversation with her.

"Are you wearing make up, Charlotte?" asks Sarah-Jane. "Looks a bit – green."

I stare at the ladybird; the eyeshadow was probably a mistake, especially now, when it must be all over my face.

"Hello," says a voice. "Lottie, isn't it?"

I look up. Sophia is standing there. She's wearing a small backpack and seems to have abandoned the rest of her stuff.

"And who are you?" demands Sarah-Jane. "How do you know Charlotte?"

Sophia smiles. "I'm Sophia. We met at her house last night," she says. She's got a clear strong voice, surprising for someone so slight.

"Ooooooh-ooo," says Sarah-Jane, doing an imitation of a siren. "You've been to Charlotte's house! No one's ever been to Charlotte's house. What's it like?"

My blood freezes. No, honestly it does, and then

it boils while I wait for Sophia to sign my death sentence.

"It's – a house," she says, quietly. "Just a house."

I breathe again and nearly cry because Sophia has just been so nice.

"Really?" asks Sarah-Jane. "How disappointing. I always thought with all that naturalist stuff it would be weird, you know, *planty*, with things growing and breeding, and yuk."

Sophia shrugs, smiles at me, then turns as Miss Sackbutt, wearing a pale yellow tracksuit and cardie, climbs on to a suitcase and clears her throat.

"Shh – everyone, everyone – girls, boys, can we quieten the chatter monster?" There's a deep silence as we all stare. Miss Sackbutt reddens, she takes off her glasses and cleans them on the corner of her cardigan. I've always had her in the Enid Blyton category, an escapee from Malory Towers; all grown up but stuck in the past. Her first name begins with an A. Agatha? Agnes?

She starts talking. "Well, thank you all. I just wanted to say a few words about safety and paying attention. Ollie, Ned, Tom!" The boys stop, stare, and shuffle their feet.

"We're off on our adventure to Bream. There will

be myself, Mr G, and Miss Wesson to accompany you."

"Miss Wesson?" mutters Sarah-Jane. "Who's she?" There's a general murmur as all the parents ask the same question.

"Miss Wesson?" calls Miss Sackbutt, and a trim woman in tight-fitting leggings and a skimpy vest springs to Miss Sackbutt's side. She's oddly tanned, like someone washed her in sunshine but forgot to do it on both sides, and I can see a tiny earpiece lodged in her hair. Maybe she's really a robot put together by a mad scientist who doesn't entirely understand how human beings work.

Beside her is a small dog. A terrier. Like its owner, it's all muscle.

Miss Wesson smiles at us. That is, her mouth smiles but her eyes don't. She jogs from foot to foot and stretches her neck like runners do before a race, while glancing around the assembled parents and children. "Hi," she says, and then as if she's suddenly aware that we're all waiting for her to say something else, she adds, "Great."

Miss Sackbutt stares at her for a millisecond too long before saying: "Miss Wesson is here for security reasons. She'll be checking that we all have a safe and enjoyable time at Bream." I can tell Miss Sackbutt is groping for things to say; it's the way she looks when she tells us a school trip has been cancelled and we're going to go pond dipping instead. "She's here to… She will, um, ensure everyone's safety while we're on the trip – away – from here."

I glance at Sophia. She's staring at Miss Wesson as if she knows her.

I look back at Miss Wesson. She's staring at Sophia in exactly the same way.

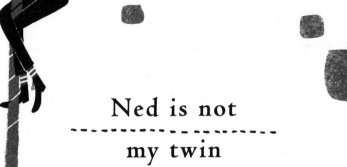

Ned is not
my twin

Buses on the whole make me vomit. Unfortunately, they have the same effect on Ned so we have to sit next to each other at the front of the coach. I'd like to make it perfectly clear at this point that Ned, although he's in the same year at school, is NOT my twin. My birthday's in September, three weeks' time in fact, and his is in August, in one week. Fate just dealt us a terrible blow, because we SHOULD be in different year groups but for one very important fortnight of the year, we're the same age.

Everyone thinks we must be twins – or, even

worse, because Ned's birthday is a fortnight before mine, they think he's my older brother. Instead he's ten about to be eleven, and I'm eleven about to be twelve.

I turn around and face the window. This coach is not a good place to be. It smells of feet, and someone's dropped a bag of gobstoppers that are rolling backwards and forwards under our seats.

I reach for *The Severed Foot*. I've just started a chapter where the hero discovers that his father is really an evil genius and has put a bomb under Big Ben, but reading on the bus'll make me sick, so instead I watch a raindrop go from the top right of the window to the bottom left. I watch another make the same journey but now I'm so bored I could just be sick from raindrop observation.

I close my eyes and think about Irene Challis. I can't quite match the image of the old lady with the veiny legs with the hero flying planes in all weathers – but then, I've probably always assumed that she was born old. I suppose all old people start off young, and even though they get covered in arthritis and old lady skin, the things they did when they were young live with them forever. I make a mental note to ask Mum about Irene's personal

things again; I'd really like to have something to remember her by.

And I don't want the pork-meat spy getting his hands on the Noah's Ark. Or handing it over to some horrible junk shop in town.

I flip round and look across the coach. Sophia is sitting next to Miss Wesson. They're both staring out of the window. Sophia looks furious.

I wonder why. But I can't ask her now.

Ned gets up and fiddles about with his bag then sits back against my hair.

"OW!" I squeal.

"Sorreeeee," he says, opening his SAS survival manual.

"It'll make you sick," I say.

"Won't," he says.

I stick my tongue out, but he ignores me. My whole family's awful. For example, Mum could have left that chicken in the shed, but no, she had to bring it in, slap it down on the kitchen table in front of Sophia and Miss Sackbutt. She did it on purpose; she's definitely trying to ruin my life. I know Sophia kept it quiet this time, but I can't expect her to stay silent for ever and Miss Sackbutt's a total blabbermouth, she'll let something slip. It won't be long before Sarah-Jane finds out, and then the whole school'll know about my dreadful home-life.

I close my eyes. No doubt I'll soon be wishing I was dead, but sleep would do for now...

"Look, there's a sheep. Look, there's a corrugated iron shed. Hey, Lottie, there's a boat just like Uncle Davy's. Look, a beach! Look, a dog – it's a chihuahua." Ned can't be quiet. It's impossible for him.

"Shut up!" I say, jamming sweet wrappers into my ears, but Ned's too loud, so I go back to staring out of the window. After twenty-seven raindrops have crossed the glass, we turn off the motorway and the landscape changes to moorland with small wooded patches. We leave the rain behind and the coach plunges down narrow-hedged lanes that brush against the windows. Finally, we burst out on to a grassy sunlit cliff, hanging over the blue sparkling sea stretching away towards France.

Miss Sackbutt struggles forward along the bus to talk to the driver and nearly sits on Ned, her huge bottom barely missing his rucksack. On her way back, she peers at Miss Wesson in the same way that she peered at the scorpion.

Miss Wesson's looking at her phone but hiding it from Sophia. She's either playing some rubbish arcade game, or sending secret codes.

They're definitely connected. I wonder if she's Sophia's personal bodyguard. Perhaps Sophia is actually a Sardinian princess and Miss Wesson fights off all unsuitable suitors.

The coach driver swings around a corner and we have to hang on to our seats. I hear Sarah-Jane not hang on to hers.

Maybe Sophia's dad just loves her so much he doesn't want her to come to any harm. I think of the elegantly suited man in our kitchen and I revise my opinion from meat spy to racehorse trainer, and then to racecourse owner.

Or he is a secret service agent and she's the living code to some terrifying discovery. In *Sandwiches for Satan* the main character's hair contains a DNA sequence code that activates the American nuclear deterrent.

I wonder. Whatever it is, I suspect that Sophia could prove to be a first class mystery. In fact, I'm sure of it.

She loves

- - - - - - - - - - - - - - - - - - -

me...

Bream Lodge is a dump. Actually, it's only half a dump because the other half slipped into the sea years ago. Since we last came, the ballroom's gone – or half gone. Someone must have built it on the cliff a hundred years ago without thinking and now all that stops you following are some flappy orange strips of plastic. It's not a lethal cliff, because it doesn't plunge straight into the water; it's a crumbly thing covered in broken toilets and half a swimming pool sliding gently to a big sandy beach.

The coach stops well away from the sea, among

the green and blue chalets. Someone's painted them up since last year, and it looks as if they've built a new assault course further inland. In fact, the whole thing seems to have moved inland, including the crumby collection of fairy lights that makes the whole place even sadder.

I wonder what Sophia thinks.

I wonder what her dad would think.

He's probably settling into his first cappuccino on the flight to New York, flashing a glance at his Rolex and selling racehorses over his iPad. Or talking to M and picking up his first assignment. Or perhaps he's already got the builders in at Irene's house and they're busy knocking through the wall of the walled garden. I'm surprised by a stab of sadness as I imagine one of the apple trees hoisted high in the air on a digger bucket.

No. It couldn't happen yet – could it?

Our mum and dad are almost certainly still trying to leave the house; in fact, they probably won't manage it for another day because it's almost impossible to find anyone to look after the hens. I lean against the window as everyone else pours off the bus, and try to work out if I'd rather be here or at home.

It's like choosing between two shades of brown.

"Come on, lazy bones!" Ned dumps my rucksack in my lap. "You want to get the best bed, don't you?"

I don't care, all the mattresses are lumpy and flea-ridden, but I lug the stupid bag off the stupid coach and drag it across the gravel. The girls are always in the blue cabins, the boys in the green, and it occurs to me that the blue cabin on the right is better because you can't hear the boys. I change tack and lug the bag faster over the grass.

Miss Wesson's dog comes with me, exploding out of a dog basket and racing between my legs. He spots something in the bushes and charges off along the cliff.

I hope very much that he and his owner are going to sleep somewhere else. I hate dogs and I don't like Miss Wesson. She's scary and he's smelly.

"Lottie," says Miss Sackbutt. "Lottie – this way." She's standing on a small concrete post, waving her arms at me. "You're in a curtained-off cubicle with me, dear, isn't that nice? Girls together."

WHAT! Someone's just chucked a bucket of imaginary iced water over my head.

WHAT? A cubicle with Miss Sackbutt? Our

beds touching, her pale yellowness rubbing off all over me. Eeeew!

"But—"

"Well, Miss Wesson thought she'd share a cubicle with Sophia as neither of them know anybody much. So I need to share a cubicle with someone, and I thought, *Charlotte* – she's the girl for me." Miss Sackbutt has this utterly stupid grin on her face.

"NO!" I say. Then, "Yes – I suppose so."

"But I don't want to share with *you!*" It's Sophia. I turn. Miss Wesson has Sophia by the elbow; she's definitely dragging her towards the cabin. Sophia is flapping her arms in an attempt to escape, but Miss Wesson appears to be made of solid oak; there's no way Sophia could escape her.

"Ah!" says Miss Sackbutt, her grin twisting into a wince. "No physical contact, Miss Wesson. Remember, dear? County-council rules? Law suits? Child abuse?"

Miss Wesson's face goes from utter incomprehension to faint understanding, and she releases Sophia. "I only thought..."

I mentally move Miss Wesson from sports-personality-turned-security-guard into Russian assassin. Either way, she's still a robot.

We follow Miss Sackbutt into the cabin. It has eight beds, four of which are behind curtains in the same way hospital beds are, except the curtains don't separate individual beds, they pair them off.

In *The Mystery of the Dead Moth*, the murderer hides a body in a curtained booth just like these. No one finds it for days.

"Perhaps," Miss Sackbutt says, looking from Miss Wesson to Sophia and then to me, "on reflection, you and I could get to know each other a little better, Miss Wesson?" Miss Sackbutt does her wide and stupid grin again and Miss Wesson stares in incomprehension. "Yes, dear, you and me." Miss Wesson's shoulders droop in acceptance. "We could take these beds, behind this curtain here. After all, what young girl wants to share with a teacher? Eh? Lump us old things in together. And get rid of these curtains here..." Miss Sackbutt pushes one lot of curtains to the side, leaving only two beds cut off from the rest of the room.

Sophia lets a broad smile spread across her face and looks almost smug for a moment. I smile, too. Miss Wesson kicks the ground, sending up a puff of dust. She's irritated, but I sense that she can't say anything back to Miss Sackbutt because Miss

44

Sackbutt's in charge. I offer an imaginary prayer of thanks for Miss S; sometimes, just sometimes, she's a bit of a marvel.

"Oh – and you'll have Sarah-Jane and Emily, too," calls Miss Sackbutt over her shoulder, picking her way across the cabin like a supermodel in a fat suit. "So make sure you leave enough space for everyone's clothes."

Sarah-Jane?

Poo.

Miss Sackbutt and Miss Wesson leave the cabin. The door swings shut, but it's light and feeble so it sits in the rectangular door frame without actually bedding down into proper shutness and I can hear Miss Sackbutt's voice as she crosses the compound towards the swimming pool. Sophia and I are alone in the cabin for about ten seconds before Sarah-Jane appears. Then Emily comes in, then Sarah-Jane leaves to look in the coach for a lost trainer and Emily unpacks a long line of teddies.

"Phew," I say, grabbing *The Severed Foot* from my bag and throwing myself on to the bed. Something occurs to me. I open the front cover of the book. There, in old-lady spidery writing, are the words *Property of Irene Challis.* So Mum's been reading Irene's books, and all the time I thought they were Mum's. I lie back and stare at the missing polystyrene tiles on the ceiling and think about Mum and Irene and wonder if there isn't something about Mum that I've missed somehow.

I roll on to my side and watch Emily arrange her teddies. She places them big to small, and then swaps them round the other way and goes small to big.

Sophia is packing her clothes into a tiny drawer; she glances up at me, and then across at Emily. I slip down from the bed and stand next to her, both of us staring into the tiny drawer. "Do you like swimming?" she whispers.

"Yes – why?"

"Talk to you later, I want to tell you something in private," she says, just as Sarah-Jane crashes in through the door and throws her trainer at my rucksack.

...She loves
me not

A few minutes later, Miss Sackbutt comes to find us. She's wearing a peachy-pink wetsuit. It's loose over the top and stretched to capacity around her bum. I didn't know such things existed, and I wondered what particularly mean shop assistant sold it to her.

"Girls, pop into your cossies, slip on some tracksuits and we'll have a go at the assault course. I gather the mud is nice and sticky!"

Was this the swimming Sophia was talking about?

Before long, we're lying in mud at the bottom of

a wall being cajoled by a man in a tracksuit. We've climbed a net, swum a canal and crawled through concrete tubes with worms all over the ceiling. It was disgusting.

We've never done the wall before; last year I suppose we were all too small. I watch as Ned and Ollie charge at it, their fingers just brushing the top, but their feet skidding off the sides. Tracksuit man thinks it's hilarious; I'd think it was pretty funny if I didn't have to do it.

It occurs to me that there's a much better way of getting over the top: Emily Cravitz used it in *No Sleep Till Cairo*, when she and Bab-el-Mar were escaping from the assassins. But I'm completely exhausted, and rather than tell anyone, I lie down and rest my hair in the mud. I dream of the shower afterwards, the lovely feeling as the hot water cuts through the dirt and leaves clean trails of skin behind. I'm imagining crisp white sheets, and shepherd's pie. Warm beds, cocoa.

In my head, I'm in a luxury hotel with fluffy white towels and views over perfectly mown lawns. If I close my eyes a little tighter I can even smell the cocoa.

"Come on, Lottie – let's do this wall." It's Sophia.

She's remarkably un-muddy, and she reaches her hand out to help me up. "I bet you know how to, don't you? You'll have worked it out."

No one's climbed it. Ned's bruised his knees trying. "You won't make it, Lottie," he sneers. "You're rubbish at this sort of thing."

I'm too tired to thump him. Instead, I make a cup with my hands. "Put your foot there, Sophia – I'll hoist you up." She clambers lightly to the top of the wall and sits astride it. I don't think she's going to be strong enough to pull me up, so I look around for the next person. Sarah-Jane? No. Emily? She's crying into Miss Sackbutt's wetsuit. Ned? Yuk. But it'll have to be, so I cup my hands.

"Result, sis!" And he pulls himself to the top. Simultaneously, he and Sophia lean down and grab my arms, lifting me easily until I teeter for a moment on the top and have to jump down the other side or fall.

It actually feels rather good. "Well done, Lottie – clever girl – co-operation is always the best way," calls Miss Sackbutt from the other side of the wall.

I look up at Sophia. She and Ned are holding hands while he lowers her from the wall.

Poo.

* * *

We're supposed to go for showers straight afterwards, but I wait for everyone to finish before I go into the shower block. I don't want anyone to see me naked. The floor is a pool of cold muddy water and I have to tiptoe to the cubicle, hang my towel on the hook and hope that it doesn't slip to the ground. I turn the shower to full power and look up. There's a slug sliding over the pale blue ceiling, right above my head. It's brown and spotty, a leopard slug like the ones in the kitchen at home.

Lovely.

The hot water streams over my hair, and the steam rises and for a few minutes I can't actually see the slug and can pretend that I'm not at scummy Bream Lodge, I'm actually in a fabulous villa in the Caribbean, meeting James Bond before going on a top secret mission. I could possibly be the double agent in *Silvergun*, the one where the Russian spy actually gets shot into space, the code tattooed on his forehead.

The moment I turn off the shower, the secret mission fades and I find myself standing in a puddle on a cold concrete floor with a slug over my head.

There's a note on my bed from Miss Sackbutt.

Lottie
The Gorge of Death. When you're ready.
Miss S.

Oh no – this is why I hate coming to Bream.

I run through the camp, up a slight hill, and arrive panting at the bottom of a rope ladder where everyone's already lined up. We did this last year – or, at least, lots of people did it last year. I got halfway up the ladder before coming down again.

The thing is, it's terrifying. The ladder seems to be made of string and a few twigs and it goes straight up a telegraph pole to a small crow's nest affair at the top. It has a rope that attaches it to another telegraph pole on the other side of a ravine. From the rope hang a series of triangles – "swings", Miss Sackbutt calls them – and beneath that, what strikes me as a ridiculously small safety net.

I wonder if Irene had to cross any tiny rope bridges when she walked across Scotland. There probably aren't any tiny rope bridges in Scotland.

They're probably all made of stone and porridge, and she would have been wearing stout brogues, not muddy second-hand trainers with sparkly bits.

And she was braver than me.

Just looking up at it makes me feel dizzy.

Tracksuit man is back, this time in a vibrant red outfit with matching red trainers.

"If you don't want to do this, I totally understand, heights aren't for everyone – but have a go, if you can."

Ned's friend, Ollie, clambers up the ladder, swings effortlessly from one triangle to the next, and reaches the far side. He seems utterly unbothered. Ned follows, skimming through the branches, placing his foot perfectly every time. He's on the other side before I can summon up a rude comment.

The queue's getting shorter. All the boys are over; now it's just the girls.

"Come on, you lot," shouts Ned from the other side. "Or are you scared?"

I could kill him. I really could.

Last year Sarah-Jane bottled out, but this year, although she struggles and tracksuit man has to climb to the top with her, she makes it over the

ravine, her face glowing with pleasure. Emily refuses to do it at all.

Miss Sackbutt smiles at me in a concerned way. Does she think I'm going to turn into a bawling baby or something? "Lottie?" she says. "Your turn."

I breathe deeply and put my foot on the first rung of the ladder. So far, so good. Then I try the second. This is OK. I look across; Miss Sackbutt's head is about level with my waist. I take another breath and climb four more rungs. And then I look down.

I can see where the dye stops and the grey begins on the top of Miss Sackbutt's head. I can see the bald patch on the top of tracksuit man's head.

I don't want to do this.

I can.

I don't want to do this.

I can.

It comes with every beat of my heart, until I reach the crow's nest. And then it stops because I am simply too scared to move.

Amanda Arnott in *Say Goodbye to Life* manages to clamber over the castle roof and she's scared of heights, but – I can't. I just can't move.

"Lottie?" calls Miss Sackbutt. "Are you all right, dear?"

I shake my head. I can't even speak.

"I'll come up," says tracksuit man.

The ladder wobbles, bending with his weight, forcing me to cling on and close my eyes, but in a second he's standing behind me, his hands on my shoulders.

"Do you want to go back down? Or go on?"

"Down," I mutter.

"OK – that's fine – you can always decide to have another go later."

I nod, and we come back down the ladder, stepping on to the solid ground that I find I have to sit on in order to hold myself together. I fix a smile on to my face, but I'd like to cry. Miss Sackbutt was right about the bawling baby.

"You can cross the ravine the easy way in a minute, when you've got your breath back," says tracksuit man, pointing at a short rope bridge stretched taut over the ravine.

"Sophia?" says Mrs Sackbutt. "How about you?"

Sophia glances at me and looks away quickly. Have I become an object of pity? "Oh me, yes of course," she says, putting her foot on the first rung.

"Shall I go up now?"

Tracksuit man nods. He looks all serious now, as if he's in the presence of greatness. In the presence of a top-flight circus gymnast.

Sophia climbs the ladder fast. Her feet fly from one rung to the next. She was born to climb high things, just like I was born not to.

She leans forward, grabs the first triangle and putting her feet on the bar, swings out towards the next.

"Bravo!" shouts Miss Sackbutt. "Well done. Keep going!"

Sophia does. She swings effortlessly over the triangles, her long black plait bouncing from her shoulder with every swing. It's rhythmical, balletic, beautiful to watch. The teachers stand below, looking up in awe.

"Bravo!" calls Miss Sackbutt again.

Sophia slips on to the crow's nest at the other end and whisks down the ladder, her feet landing lightly on the ground and completing the impression of a circus gymnast.

She crosses the little rope bridge that hangs over the ravine, "the easy way," and comes to stand next to me. There's a ripple of polite applause, and sighs of admiration.

"So clever, so impressive," says Miss Sackbutt, slapping Sophia on the back. "Wonderful to have you with us."

I feel rubbish.

That night, I dream I have to climb a mountain. It has a narrow crumbling path, with a tiny wire handrail and a bottomless cloud-filled chasm to the side. At the end of the path, a ladder goes straight up into clouds; for some stupid reason, I always climb it, only to find that I've got to go down another vertical ladder, back through the clouds and over a valley hundreds of feet below. This time, Mum's there, brandishing the chicken, a mad light in her eye. She's behind me, telling me not to be a wimp, telling me to get on with it; behind her is ancient Irene, dressed in her RAF uniform and holding another chicken in her lumpy hands. I look forward and there's Ned, skipping down the ladder easily, laughing and talking as he goes. I turn and start to descend, my feet slipping on the rungs.

I hate heights.

My foot slips, I let go, and fall...

Come on
----
in...

"Lottie!"

Something is happening to my shoulder. Someone's shaking it. That's odd, because normally Ned just bellows in my ear if he needs to wake me up.

Perhaps it isn't Ned.

"Lottie."

I open my eyes. It's dark, but it's not utterly dark, and my bedroom seems to have changed shape.

"Lottie."

I follow the arm up to the head. I can't work out who it is.

"What?"

"Shhh – it's Sophia. Put on your swimsuit."

"What?"

"We're going for a swim."

"Now? But it's the middle of the night – isn't it?"

"It's four o'clock. C'mon."

The figure glides through the cabin, and a faint rectangle of light appears around the door. I fumble in the dark, pulling on my damp costume, snapping the elastic over my shoulders and hoisting up the baggy legs. I'm ridiculously tired, so my arms and legs move but my brain's still asleep on the pillow.

I pad across the floor and out of the door. It's before dawn so there's only a little light, enough to show shapes but not colours. Over in the woods creatures rustle but here in Bream Lodge, nothing's moving.

I stop and nestle my foot into the damp earth, and look up. The sky's all different, not at all like it was when we went to bed. I can see Orion; I'm sure Dad said it was a winter constellation.

"C'mon, Lottie – this way."

From where I'm standing, Sophia's head is all mixed up with the silhouettes of the trees, but when a large bush makes a run for it, I know it's

her and follow.

Behind me something rummages in the grass. A giant rat?

"Stop here." We're by a tall black thing. I put my fingers out and brush it with my fingertip. It's a fence. I think I've finally woken up enough to realise what we're doing.

"Sophia — we'll get into big trouble for this."

"We won't get caught. Now — the way we did the wall — put out your hand."

"Wha–?" But I do put out my hand, and although I can't see a thing, I feel her foot in my fingers and her other foot on the top of my head before there's a jolt and a thump on the other side, and then silence.

"Sophia?" I whisper.

Something rattles, and the big dark patch develops a pale hole as Sophia opens the gate in the fence.

"Come in — welcome to our private swimming pool."

The tiles are cold and dry, but I catch a whiff of chlorine as Sophia tugs at the cover. It crunches as she pulls and the water slops in the pool. It's all very black.

SPLASH!

"Sophia?" I call.

White rings appear on the surface and in the middle, a blacker blob.

"Come in, it's deliciously warm."

I sit, dangling my legs over the side. I wouldn't call it warm, more freezing, but I lower myself until the water reaches my waist and my feet brush the bottom.

"Isn't it heavenly?" she says.

I lean forward, the water slopping in through the top of my cossie.

"It's cold," I say. "And how are we going to get back in without Miss Sackbutt spotting wet footprints?"

"Stop worrying," says Sophia. "Lean back, float… dream. We're free."

But I can't help worrying. I'm never in trouble. I hate being in trouble, it makes me feel ill, but then I don't want to lose Sophia, either, so I try to relax and lean back. The stars are fading overhead and the sky's gathering a kind of greeny-blue colour, but I'm not enjoying the beauty – I'm feeling sick instead. My hair soaks up the water, then I remember it'll give me away so I yank it out with a splash which worries me because it makes so much noise and I have to scramble out of the water before I drown myself and sit on the side, shivering.

"What were you going to tell me?" I say.

"Oh – I don't know, it doesn't matter." Her voice is flat.

"I sort of want to know now," I say. "Something's going on, isn't it?"

There's a long silence while Sophia swims over to the side. "I'm worried," she says. "Worried about landing you with it all."

I look at her head; I might be looking into her eyes but it's too dark to tell. "All what?"

Sophia sighs. "Everything. All of it. It's complicated."

I pull my knees up and breathe hot air on to them.

"Tell me," I say.

"Are you sure?"

I nod, then realise that she can't see my head. "Yes."

She takes a deep breath. "My name is Sophia Formosa—"

"I thought it was Pinhead?"

"He – the 'Pinhead' – is not my dad. He's not

even my proper stepfather. He married my mum years ago in an illegal ceremony in Thailand, to which I wasn't invited. Since then, I've been in boarding school after boarding school while he and Mum trot round the world."

I revise my opinion of Pinehead back to racehorse trainer, then to pork-meat spy, touch on bouncer before looking for something darker still. Paid assassin? "That's rough. Why so many schools?"

Sophia laughs. "I keep getting expelled! I managed to break the rules in each one until they asked me to leave. I've run away three times. I just wanted to get back to Mum, but Pinehead keeps on finding me and finding more schools."

"Expelled? I've never met anyone who's been expelled." I sit in silence, digesting the news that this tiny, innocent-looking person has managed to get herself expelled and more than once. I'm not sure if I'm in awe or just horrified.

"It's easy – if you try hard enough – and believe me, I've tried. But that's not the point. I get myself thrown out of the schools so that I can get home. Pinehead hasn't let me see my mum for two years, no, actually it must be five; not since they got married, anyway. He's keeping us apart."

"What? But why? Why would he do that?"

"Because – because…" Sophia pauses, swooshing her foot in the pool. "He hates her, he hates me. He wants to make us both miserable, and, he's a fraudster."

"That's so… so…" I want to say exciting – but just stop myself in time.

"He wants her money – there's plenty of it; he's in love with someone else, and Mum's in the way…" She finishes quietly, sounding infinitely sad.

"Blimey," I say.

"It's that Wesson woman. She's the one he's having an affair with. I know, but my mother doesn't. I need to tell her about them – and the money."

I listen to the water plopping back into the pool, absorbing everything Sophia has told me. I want to say: *It sounds like* The Savage Night *and you sound like Tina Temper – catgirl extraordinaire – fighting against the forces of evil*, but instead I say: "I thought Miss Wesson was something to do with you. We've never had anyone like her come to Bream before."

"Yes. She appeared a few months ago, they—"

Sophia stops, listens. "Shhh."

There are voices, and rattling, and only just enough time to slip back into the pool.

Unfortunately, the voices have a big torch, water's see-through, and they shine it right at me.

Last seen
wearing...

Miss Sackbutt is rubbish at telling people off. I don't know why I've always been so frightened of it.

"And Charlotte – you shouldn't do things like this, you know, you nearly gave me a heart attack. Miss Wesson waking me like that in the night, peeling back my eye shades and shining a torch – well!" Miss Sackbutt flaps her hand in front of her face as if she's having another near heart attack.

"And so unexpected – YOU? The most sensible child in the class, of all children! It was the dog that found you, of course – clever little thing."

I sit very still and hope it will blow over, which it does in about a minute, and before I've even had a chance to do tears and beg forgiveness she's given me a piece of her KitKat.

Miss Wesson tells off Sophia. I don't know what she says but Sophia's face is red and puffy afterwards, as if she did do tears, and I don't think there was any KitKat-sharing.

We have to sit separately at breakfast and Miss Wesson gets between us afterwards, so I can't talk to Sophia even when we're walking down to the wetsuit sheds although I'm dying to find out more about her mum, Pinhead and Wesson.

"Who's done it before?" asks tracksuit man, pointing at a kayak.

Everyone puts their hands up, except for me. Ned shoots me a glance. I have done it before, but I'm no good at it; I'd rather everyone thought I was a complete beginner.

It turns out Sophia is rather excellent at kayaking – one of her schools was on the shore of Lake Superior in Canada – so tracksuit man puts us together.

"But—" says Miss Wesson, her mouth open in disbelief.

"It's a health and safety issue, Miss Wesson," says tracksuit man. "I can't send Charlotte out there on the sea without an experienced kayaker and I need to keep the instructors in boats on their own, so…" He shrugs and picks up a life jacket from the beach.

I send Miss Wesson a bright smile and she scowls back, but then she climbs into her kayak and waits for us to launch.

Sophia gets to sit in the back, steering, while I'm in the front, as "the engine". The boat smells of old wellington boots, as does the wetsuit, but I lower myself in until the wetsuit cuts off my circulation and the lifejacket blocks my nose and mouth. Once the helmet's on too, I can barely see, move or breathe.

"Brilliant," says tracksuit man. "Sea's nice and calm, see how you get on, paddle out towards the yellow buoy and then back to the orange one."

We launch, and Miss Wesson launches a millisecond afterwards, the bow of her kayak bobbing along beside us. We leave her dog on the shore, barking.

I try very hard, but I don't think I'm a natural. The yellow buoy turns out to be miles away and before very long I'm sweating, and the sandy bits in the wetsuit are rubbing my armpit, and the stupid helmet's slipped and is dangling over one eye. I can see the front of our boat but that's about it. After a short burst of rain, the sun comes out and boils the water that's fallen inside my wetsuit. If you like the feeling of sitting in warm wee, then it's nice. If not, don't go kayaking.

Sophia is talking to me but because of the stupid lifejacket I can't hear her properly.

I run through the plot of *Last Stand in Paradise*. The hero's just swum the river, and he's exhausted, and three more trained assassins spring out of the bush...

"Five more minutes," shouts tracksuit man. Everyone seems to be racing now, kayaks are whizzing across our bow, the water's white with mad paddling.

I start to count.

One chimpanzee, two chimpanzees...

Back in Last Stand in Paradise the hero grabs at a piece of bamboo, sweeping the assassins off their feet... This is taking forever.

Five chimpanzees, six chimpanzees.

Someone clips our stern heading towards the

68

yellow buoy at speed.

"Hey!" shouts Sophia.

Nine chimpanzees, ten chimpanzees, eleven chimpanzees...

"Ow! You idiot!"

I crane my neck round to see who shouted, nearly decapitating myself on the sharp edge of the lifejacket. Miss Wesson's boat's gone. Sophia swings the boat around so that we can see what's happened. The motorboat seems to be next to a pair of kayaks, but someone's in the water and one of the kayaks seems to be upside down. All the other kayaks are charging towards it.

Tracksuit man's standing, shouting in the motorboat, and, just as the overturned kayak starts to right itself, we see him dive into the water.

I try to keep it in view, but I find keeping anything still about the kayak almost impossible.

"Quick!" Sophia yells. "Just paddle as hard as you can – I'll steer!"

Without thinking I paddle like a maniac, trying to copy what other people's arms have been doing, which is far more efficient than the thing that my arms have been doing. We whizz back towards the shore and then skirt around some rocks. The sea's slightly rougher here but Sophia steers through it, and I try to keep up the speed. It's all hard work and the stupid helmet means that I can only just see the rocks bobbing in front of me.

"Sophia," I shout. "Sophia, slow down!" I can't look back to see where we've come from, the lifejacket would saw my head off, but I can just about see where we're going.

To my huge relief, she rams the boat on to a sandy gap in the rocks, wriggles and clambers out, before grabbing me and hauling me out of the boat.

"Well done, Lottie," she cries. "Are you OK?"

I nod – I can't answer, I'm too out of breath – so I lie for a moment staring at the sky. A bank of cloud is approaching from the sea and I can just make out the ragged edge of rain that must be coming our way.

"Sophia," I breathe. "What have we done? What are we doing?"

"Escaping," she says.

"Oh," I say. I'd like to add, "I want you to be my friend but I wasn't expecting this," but instead I say, "Of course. But is this a good way of doing it?"

"I want to see my mum. She's in the country, for a week – I have to talk to her..." Her voice fades away. Then, "Come on," she says briskly. "We need

to hide this boat." She scrapes the sand away on either side of the kayak so that it sinks into the beach.

I stand watching her, absorbing the leg-shaking enormity of what we've done. "But Sophia — we've just run away, by boat."

"Yes." She turns and looks up at me. "I know. And thanks."

"But I haven't entirely agreed to it yet," I say, struggling with the wet straps and tearing off the beastly life jacket.

She doesn't say anything, just looks up at me, and I can see that her eyes are brimming with tears.

"Oh, all right, I promise I'll help, but this is insane, you do know that?" I say, pulling the boat into a hollow in the sand and dumping a wodge of seaweed over it. I crouch down to join her, taking off my helmet and using it to dollop sand on to the kayak.

"Brilliant," she says, copying me. "This is my only chance to see Mum, tell her what's going on... And I knew you were the right person to bring."

"Not Ned, then?" I say, thinking of them sitting on the top of the wall, hand in hand, or skipping along cliff tops, careless of the drop below.

"Ned?" she laughs. "Why Ned?"

"No reason," I say, allowing a tiny light of hope to flicker in my heart. A light that says that just as she means something to me, I mean something to her. "Just wondered."

"There's no one else who I can trust and who's capable of it." She looks with her almost black eyes into mine. The tiny light of hope becomes a steady flame. "Can you imagine Sarah-Jane doing this?" she asks.

I think of Sarah-Jane in my place, complaining, sitting helpless on the sand, clamouring for attention. Then in my mind's eye I see me, a strong silent me striding alongside Sophia, guiding her, giving wisdom to her in her mission. A heroic me. "No."

"Exactly."

We probably spend about ten minutes hiding the boat. When we've finished, we pile rocks and more seaweed on the disturbed sand, and watch as a sudden squall blows in from the sea and the rain destroys our footprints.

"Brilliant," Sophia says, flicking her dripping plait to the side. "Let's get going."

"Have you got a plan?" I ask, following her

over the rocks.

"We need to get to Mum before Pinhead finds us. This way, I think," she says.

It's not exactly a plan, I think but don't say, as we scramble over boulders and through three small bays that nestle beneath the cliffs.

Soon, the mist that was out at sea rolls in towards us, and I can barely see my arm in front of my face.

"How far are we going?" I ask, out of breath. "Is this a long escape or a short escape?"

Sophia doesn't reply, but I can hear her feet on the stones in front of me, and I follow them through to another sandy bay.

"Sophia?" I ask. I'm just beginning to feel anxious. I'm not sure whether I want to see a coastguard helicopter scouring the sea for us, or whether I don't. It slightly depends on what Sophia is thinking of doing. I want to be a hero but what is there to eat, for example, or drink?

Flowers for
Sophia

We stumble on for another hour or so, until the coastal path comes down to meet the shore. An orange boat appears just out to sea, joined soon after by a helicopter. We hide under a pile of nets until they go away, before walking some more.

In *Rendezvous at West Point*, Dr Tabitha Cross walks twenty-seven miles along rocks before wrestling her evil stepmother to the ground. Difference is, Dr Tabitha Cross was fit and wore shoes. My feet hurt and I'm out of breath.

She also had some idea of where she was going.

A couple walk past with their dog, and we collapse

74

on to the rocks in our wetsuits as if we were just out for a swim. I'm completely starving, breakfast was a really long time ago and if someone offered me one of Dad's homemade squirrel sausages, I might even consider eating it.

We must be about six miles away from Bream by now.

I'm tempted to wander over to the couple and ask to use their mobile phone, but I glance at Sophia and lose heart. She's looking really determined. She's also looking like she might cry.

"Sophia," I ask gently, "what exactly are we doing?"

She's silent as a group of ramblers wander on to the beach and start chucking pebbles into the sea.

"We're going to find Mum."

"And where is she?"

She sits in silence, spinning stones across the beach.

"I think — I don't know exactly."

I've never been very good at whistling between my teeth, but it comes out sufficiently loud to make one of the ramblers turn sharply and fling a stone at his friend by accident. "So where do we start? Why don't you tell me something about her?

What does she do?"

"She's a singer…"

"Would I have heard of her?"

"Doubt it – she mostly performs in other countries – that's why she's never here. In fact I only know she's here at the moment because I heard Wesson and Pinhead talking about her on the way down here. But that doesn't matter. The point is that Pinhead knows where she is, so if we can get to his office, we can find out where she's performing. If we get there soon, we can get to her first."

"Couldn't you just email her or something?"

Sophia shakes her head. "I don't have her email address. Pinhead's never given it to me, and he tries to send me to school in remote places where the internet doesn't work. That's why he sent me to Bream Lodge. Out of sight, and out of contact – he always wants me well out of the way."

I thought everywhere had the internet these days, except for us, of course, but I pick weed from between my toes and try to imagine how I'd feel if I was kept away from my mum, how I'd feel if someone wanted to take all her money and I knew about it and she didn't.

"If he wanted to defraud her, wouldn't he do it miles away, in the Cayman Islands or somewhere?"

Sophia draws a heart in the sand. "He's got cronies here. This is his turf."

"Oh," I say. This is a world I thought I knew about from my books. But perhaps I don't.

"Of course, she could be dead," says Sophia. "That could be why I haven't seen her for years."

"Surely you'd know if she was," I say. "You'd have been told at school, you know, like in *The Twelve Fish Scales,* where Sarah Turnbull gets called into the Head's office and told her parents have been killed in a terrible airship-meets-herd-of-cows calamity."

She sniffs. "He might have kept it a secret from the school, too."

"Oh!" I say. I can't think of anything else. I throw some pebbles at a can, and miss.

"We could go back, get the police to investigate?" I say. "Tell them your mum's missing, that you haven't seen her in – what was it? Five years?"

"NO!" says Sophia, her face twisted with anger and tears. "They wouldn't believe us, and he'd hide the evidence – I have to do it myself; if you want to leave I'll just go on, alone…"

"Where's his office?" I ask, looking around at the almost empty beach as if Pinhead's office might be just round the corner, but really I'm dreading the answer.

"Bristol."

"That's quite a long way away," I say, imagining the journey stretching across a map of the South West. "Maybe a hundred and fifty miles?" We sit in a long contemplative silence while I think about whether I can be hero enough to carry Sophia through all this, and help her find the truth.

I remember Irene, and the plane crash. She was alone, in a cold fog, hundreds of miles from home. "Do you know anything about Irene Challis?" I ask.

"Irene Challis?"

"She's the old woman that died and left her house to Pinhead."

Sophia shakes her head. "Never heard of her – I don't know anything about his relatives – I don't think he has any. I don't think anyone could be related to anything as vile as Pinhead."

"No, he does sound – unpleasant. What does he do? Except for dabbling in property development and keeping people apart?"

"Import and Export – that's what he says to

people. But I think he's a gun runner."

My mouth suddenly dries up. *A gun runner?* And I'd thought he was something to do with pork.

Do I have enough of an inner hero? Can I, like Scarface McCready in *The Secret of the Lost Uncle*, do good in the face of extreme danger, unrecognised, warmed by the inner knowledge of extreme selflessness in the cause of justice and friendship? I feel a surge of righteous power and my little flame of courage bursts into a raging fire; Sophia needs me, she needs me to help her do SOMETHING EXCITING. Just me; only me.

I'm thinking of the changed me, the *something happened to me*, that I'll have afterwards. It'll be awesome.

"I'm hungry," says Sophia. "And thirsty."

Apart from our wetsuits, there really isn't anything to eat, but if I'm going to be Sophia's heroic best friend I need to find something. I look around. The beach is pebbly; at the top, some sad plants with yellow flowers struggle on the edge of a sandy cliff. I wander over. They're that sea broccoli stuff – Dad once cooked it down at Portland with mackerel; it was disgusting, but it's food.

Raw food.

I pick the flowers and try one. It tastes like cabbage. Peppery, disgusting, but not inedible. I bring back some flowers for Sophia.

She sticks one in her mouth and chews. I expect her to choke, or spit it out, but she says: "Thank you, Lottie. Thank you."

The affair of the
giant lobster

We struggle on until it gets dark and decide to camp under an upturned rowing boat. Things crawl all around us, poppy things that crunch if you walk on the sand. They're probably edible if you could catch them, and if you had a cooking pot.

And a fire.

And some salt and pepper.

And water.

We huddle together in our wetsuits, listening for footsteps and feeling hungry. We've eaten sea-cabbage flowers, sorrel leaves and the end of a piece of bread that some picnickers left on the beach.

Apart from a tap for washing sand from wetsuits, we haven't found any water, and I'm not sure we should have drunk from it but bad water seems preferable to no water.

My stomach rumbles for the millionth time. I'm thinking about chocolate bars. I can't help it; they keep coming into my head. I've had a particularly strong sense of Swiss chocolate bunnies, the ones wrapped in gold paper. Ned can't bear them, he says it's like eating happiness, so I always save him from that by eating his too. "What would you really like to eat just now?" I blurt out.

"Spaghetti con vongole," Sophia says. "With loads of parmesan."

"Oh," I say, not wanting to show my ignorance by asking what it is. "I'd settle for chocolate."

We sit in silence, listening to the crunching things on the beach. I imagine they're probably eating each other. I pull my legs in closer. I daren't lie down, I don't want the sea things to move into my hair.

There's a bit in *Sand for Sandy,* where Sandy has to battle with an enormous crab. She kills it with an umbrella. It's quite dramatic and heroic.

But just at the moment, I'm not feeling very

heroic, and I don't have an umbrella.

"I wonder if my parents know yet?" I ask.

"They'll have rung them straight away. They always ring Pinhead the moment I take off."

"Ours are off camping in Cornwall – they probably didn't take a mobile phone."

"Really?" asks Sophia. "I didn't think anyone went anywhere without a phone."

I shrug. "My parents are different."

"They are," says Sophia. "I liked them."

"Oh!" I say, feeling a confusing sense of pride and embarrassment. "That's——"

"I've lived all over the world, I can speak three languages, I've had nannies, and minders, and stayed in hotels on my own, but I've never met anyone like your parents – or you, for that matter."

"Really?"

"You go swimming in that crummy old bathing suit, and you don't mind; you wear turquoise eyeshadow; you bring an enormous ancient rucksack on a school trip; you've got sensible socks, sensible shoes, sensible trousers. You actually read books! It's great that you're so unbothered."

The blush starts somewhere near the bottom of my spine though I make a mental note *never* to wear makeup again. Sophia might be completely wrong about how unbothered I am but I still want to hug her, though I don't think I know her quite well enough yet.

Somewhere not very far away, a dog barks.

"How did Pinhead and your mum meet?" I ask, whispering this time, like I might set the dog off.

"When she started singing, he was her manager."

I imagine Sophia's mum as a slender blonde, crooning into a microphone.

"So they fell in love?"

Sophia goes silent for a long time, so long that I think she might have fallen asleep, and I finally slip down so that my hair lies on the sand.

"I don't think she fell in love with him."

"Did he fall in love with her?"

There's a long pause while the things outside eat each other.

"I think he realised he could control her – and she liked having someone to organise everything for her. I think I was the problem from the start, but it was all different then, because Mum and I lived on our own in a little flat in Maida Vale, over the tube station, where the trains shook the bookcases and the rats ran around at night."

"Nice," I say, changing my vision to one where Sophia's mum, still slender and blonde, is standing at the top of the stairs batting away the rats with a frying pan.

"We had cockroaches, too, but I used to keep them as friends under the bed in a box; my cockroaches never ran away with all the others, they stayed."

"Really?"

"I loved it there," she says. "Just me and Mum, and I went to a local school and had lots of friends, and wore a red-and-white checked dress. And then he turned up, and the two of us started to live separate lives – me at boarding school and her performing around the world. She's sung at the Paris Opera House, you know, and in Sydney." Sophia sighs loudly.

"I thought he wanted her money?"

"Mum never had any money then but she's earned squillions since. He's in charge of it, and he must have spent loads on my education."

Something crunches really close by, and I sit absolutely still for a moment. It's probably a giant lobster eating a giant crab. Unless it's a giant cockroach.

"So what does he say when you tell him you want

to see your mum?"

"That she's ill or in Australia or something. Or taking a health cure."

"Aren't there any friends you could ask about her – *her* friends, I mean?"

"She doesn't have any anymore – all her old friends have fallen away. I've tried but they don't know anything. Not the ones I can find, anyway."

"What about the internet – can't you find anything out about her?"

"Oh – I've tried looking for her on the web. I can't find her, but he says she's changed her name."

"Oh," I say. I thought you could find anything out on the internet, even people with changed names, but then, I don't really know anything about it – I've only ever used it at school, to look stuff up for history projects. Sophia's bound to be right.

"He *made* her change her name. He's like that."

Something's bugging me. "Actually – I thought you said he kept you away from the internet, so that you couldn't contact her?"

"Oh, he does, but I've found out about her through other people, people who have been able to use computers. You know, teachers and people…"

We sit in the relative silence of sea things crackling outside.

"What was her name? Before he made her change it?"

"Isadora."

"Isadora what?"

"Oh. Fonseca."

"Fonseca?" I say. "But yours is Formosa."

"Yes – they're different. I'm named after my father – he was a Spanish sea captain. Died in a tsunami. Unless he's still alive on a desert island somewhere— What's that noise? Outside?"

Something else crunches outside the boat – either that or the same lobster's found another crab – or do crabs eat lobsters? Or do cockroaches eat both?

We sit stock still. I listen intently until it feels like my ears are going to burst.

It sounds like two lobsters now. Really big ones.

"Heloooooooo! Girls!"

And someone pulls the boat off from over our heads.

The uninvited
guest

It's Ned. And I can't work out if I'm glad or furious. While I'm still thinking about it, he snuggles down under the side of the boat and starts talking.

"Need to hide from the helicopters — have they been this far along the coast?" He shines his torch in my eyes.

"Ned! Torch!" I squeal.

"Oh — sorry. But did you see the crash? I sank the Wesson woman with one blow — she's totally rubbish at steering — but the noise was spectacular, and I did think I might possibly have drowned

88

her, but the course leader dived in to get her out, although she was already out, so they were both wet by then – and," Ned coughs, "really cross. Anyway, the motorboat rescued her, Miss Sackbutt told me off which was like being told off by a bathmat, and it took them all that time to work out that you two had gone, and only I had seen which direction you went in."

"But how did you know we wanted to escape?" asks Sophia. "Sorry, *I* wanted to escape."

"I didn't. It was a complete accident. I was watching a cormorant landing on a buoy, and I hit Wesson. She's not very lovely. She is here because of you, Sophia, isn't she?"

"Of course she is!" I snap, now feeling that my heroic stance is being eroded by the chivalrous actions of my unchivalrous brother. "So why are you here?"

"I didn't think you'd want to be on your own for ever. I mean, it's not possible to be out here with only a wetsuit for very long. You can't exactly buy anything, or ask for anything, or even hide, and at some point, your skin'll fall off."

"What?" asks Sophia.

"He's probably right," I say, reluctantly. "A

wetsuit is like wearing a wet rubber glove. After a while, things get fetid."

"Eeeew," says Sophia.

"I knew it," cheers Ned. "I knew she'd be an 'Eeeew' girl. Just like you."

"She's not," I say. "She lived in a flat full of rats."

"Oh, I heard that bit. Do you believe it?" Ned asks me as though Sophia's not there, and starts pulling something out of his bag.

"I do," I say, reaching out my hand to grasp Sophia's wrist in a gesture of solidarity.

"Hmmm," says Ned, chucking something at me.

"What's this?" I ask.

"Clothes," says Ned. "Out of the lost property box. And what about the bit about her mum being a singer?"

"But she is," says Sophia.

I wriggle to reach the zip of the wetsuit. "What you don't know is that Sophia thinks that Pinhead – Pinehead – wants to keep her away from her mum, so that he can steal her mum's fortune." I say it firmly, unpeeling the warm rubber suit and reaching for what appears to be a T-shirt.

"Really?" says Ned. "Sounds like something out of one of your books, Lottie."

I thump him, and drag on some tracksuit bottoms.

"But we don't know she hasn't made it all up, all the sea captain bit, the gun running, and the names," says Ned.

"What about Miss Wesson, then?" I say.

"She might be exactly what Miss Sackbutt said, just someone hired by the school for extra security."

"But it's all true..." mutters Sophia in the dark, her voice quiet but with a hint of a sob. She's rustling. Pulling clothes on over her head.

"Oh, I'm not saying it isn't but we like proof in our family, don't we, Lottie?"

"You do," I say. "I..." I don't know what to say. I'm just glad it's dark and no one can see the colour of my face.

We sit in silence. I know Ned's got a point but I don't want him to be right. I want Sophia to be my friend, not his, and although he's right about the wetsuits, and the proof, and the running away on our own, I could happily feed his unromantic and boringly practical brain to the giant lobster.

"Anyway," says Ned breezily, "it doesn't matter either way – it's fun being here, on the run, under an upturned boat and now you're both properly dressed, we should sleep so that we can set off really early."

"But we haven't eaten anything," I say.

"Ah – food – thought you might want some. Here…" There's rustling as Ned pulls something else from his backpack. "Sophia, take the torch."

Our boat tent fills with light and the warm smell of sausages as Ned spreads a bundle of tinfoil on his knees. There are two long hot dog sausages. Normally, I'd say they were disgusting. I really do think they look like poo, but just at the moment, my instinct is to grab both and cram them into my mouth, but then I remember Sophia and say: "You first." I watch, my tongue hanging out, as she takes the first sausage and nibbles it.

"Lottie?" says Ned.

"Oh – I'm not really hungry—"

"In that case…" Ned lifts the tinfoil up towards his mouth.

"No!" I scream, grabbing the sausage just before his nose touches it.

"Ha!" he says. "I knew it!"

"Ned!" I say, tearing at the soft salty flesh of the sausage. "You really are…"

"…very kind to come and find us with a warm

dinner?" he says, folding the tinfoil and putting it carefully back into his rucksack. "Water anyone?"

This time, I grab the bottle first but as it turns out, Ned's brought two.

"So anyway – I followed your tracks."

"Our tracks? But we went along the coast, on purpose, so that we couldn't leave any tracks."

"Yes, but you buried a boat – I found it; no one else knows – then you clambered over the rocks with sandy feet; a little further on I found two wetsuit bum prints in the sand and a load of sea-cabbage stalks. Then there was the tap, which had obviously been used and was after all the only water, and then, this boat had to be the only place that you could possibly hide. After all, where else could you go in a swimsuit?" Even though I can't see it, I can imagine his horrid grin – he's so SMUG!

"Well done, Ned. You're either very good at tracking, or we're lousy at hiding our tracks," says Sophia, licking her lips. "What about everyone else?"

"They think you've gone the other way – I don't know why, but it might be because I told them you were looking for Mum and Dad in Cornwall, and for some reason I don't understand Sarah-Jane said she'd seen you go that way too."

I imagine Sarah-Jane pointing in the wrong direction with certainty. It would be just like her to do that because it would make her important. For a moment I feel sorry for Sarah-Jane, but then I remember just how unpleasant she is and stop.

Overhead we hear the thump of a helicopter. We switch off the torch and sit motionless under the boat, waiting for it to pass. In fact, the helicopter stays in the area for so long that I think it must have seen us but in the end it turns and goes back along the coast.

"Flip!" says Ned, after it's gone. "That was close."

Attempted

murder

Sleep comes slowly, but the morning seems to come too fast. I wake, strange sounds come from outside the boat, not giant prawn-eating lobster noises, more like chicken noises. I lift the side of the boat. Ned's standing there, proudly holding a hen. A living hen, under his arm.

"Breakfast!" he says.

"Where did you get her?" I ask.

Ned nods over his shoulder away from the sea. "Farm – up there."

"You're not really going to kill her? Are you?" Sophia asks, creeping out behind me, her eyes round.

"Why not? Mum does it all the time."

"Yes, but have *you* ever done it?" I ask.

Ned sort of nods his head, then turns it into a shake. "Well, no, not actually, not as such – I've seen it happen, though."

"Go on then." I scramble out into the half-light.

Ned takes the chicken's head in one hand and holds the rest of the bird in the other. She tilts her head and looks up at his hand as if it's going to give her something interesting to eat. Sophia covers her eyes and turns back towards the boat.

I'm not sure if I want him to succeed or not. I'm not sure that even if he managed to do it, I could eat it.

Ned stares at his hand. He stares at the hen. I suspect he's holding his breath because his shoulders are hunched with extreme concentration.

He sighs. "No, not today, henny penny," he says, putting her gently on the pebbles. She responds by pecking at his shoes, lowering her bum and laying a small brown egg.

Ned picks it up immediately. "Result!" We all gaze at the egg as if we've never seen one before. "I'll put it somewhere safe," he says, pulling a tin

mug and a small take-away box out of his bag.

"What is *that* in there?" asks Sophia, staring at the box. "Looks like slugs."

"Pinky and Perky," says Ned, clicking off the top.

Two fat Roman snails lift their heads, waiting for food.

"Why are they here?" I ask, tweaking the baggy legs of my tracksuit.

"Because if I'd left them behind, I'd have had to tell Ollie to look after them and that would have given the game away." He wraps the egg in a sock and stows it in the mug, before rummaging for a lettuce leaf from a sandwich bag and feeding it to the snails.

"WHAT?" I say, staring at the perfectly good green lettuce leaf going into the slimy box. "You're feeding them when we're starving?"

"They're my pets, I have to look after them first."

"They'd have survived," I say, swapping my socks over.

"They might have died, and I would have felt guilty," says Ned. "Anyway, they've got nothing to do with you – they're my responsibility. Here, have some trainers. I don't know if they'll fit."

He throws four shoes on to the pebbles. I look up at Sophia, elegant in a long green skirt-cum-shorts thing and a matching top, and then back at myself. An orange sweatshirt and faded navy tracksuit bottoms.

Ned studies us both. "Sorry," he says. "They were the best I could find. And, Lottie, it was orange or pink and I knew you wouldn't want pink. So…" He shrugs. "Anyway, no one's going to see you."

A princess
castle

"Did I tell you that Pinhead was a murderer?" asks Sophia as we drop down into yet another valley.

"Do you mean like – killed someone? On purpose?"

"Yes – in a fight – in a pub, or was it a restaurant?"

We both stare at her.

"That's awful," says Ned.

"Really?" I say. "He actually killed someone?"

Sophia looks away. "Yes, it was ... too awful."

We pick our way through a bog. Personally, I'm scared. Discovering that Pinhead actually has killed someone changes my view of this whole thing, but

I don't want the others to know. I want them to think I'm brave.

Daphne Downs in *Night of Crime* keeps going even though she's so scared her heart stops.

Although, I don't quite understand how that's possible.

Sophia doesn't seem to know who Pinhead killed.

"Some bloke," she says. "I expect he owed him money. It's usually about money, isn't it?"

"Or love," I say. "Although in *Death Among the Lilies* the murderer says he did it because he liked killing things. Perhaps Pinhead likes killing things?"

"Flip," says Ned. "Hope he makes an exception for kids."

"Was it just one person?" I ask.

Sophia doesn't answer for ages. "I'm not sure," she says in the end.

We struggle down the cliff on to another beach and start walking east along the edge of the surf so that our footsteps vanish. In *Canada by Gaslight* the heroine walks the whole of the west coast to keep from being tracked.

Or was it the east coast?

"Are you sure he killed someone?" asks Ned, emptying water from his shoe.

"Yes – well, I think so," says Sophia. "He went to prison for it."

"Flip," says Ned again.

In the distance, the turrets of a castle appear against the horizon.

"It looks like a princess castle," says Sophia. "My mother's a princess."

"Is she?" I ask. "Really?"

"Yes, really. Princess of some Italian place, I can't remember where. It's exactly the sort of place you might find a princess." She points at the turrets.

"Or a prince – a handsome prince," I say.

"Oh yeah," says Ned. "There's a handsome prince sitting in his tower window waiting for you, blowing kisses across the sand. 'Ah, come here Charlotte, my lovely – I have been imprisoned here for years, release me...'"

Sophia laughs.

I could happily push them both into the sea, run back, tell Miss Wesson where Sophia is, go home to my skanky bedroom, stick my inner hero into a box under the bed and listen to Lurve FM until my ears fall off.

And I'm hungry – so hungry, my stomach's eaten itself. I wonder if sand's edible?

But then I think about Pinhead, the murderer, keeping Sophia and her mother apart, and carry on putting one foot in front of the other.

"If you're really lucky he'll see you wearing those fantastic trousers!" laughs Ned, and clutches his sides theatrically.

Sophia stops laughing and stares at the ground, but I know she thinks I look ridiculous. I do, I simply do and she looks fantastic in that skirt-shorts thingy.

I trek on across the sand and do my best to ignore Ned, but he's slipped back into pondlife in my cast of characters. Something single cell and slimy with no eyes.

I hate him.

I'm not sure what I think about Sophia.

It takes an age to reach the rocks at the foot of the castle walls. They shoot up vertically from the ground and there's no way we can do anything but walk around them until the beach seems to dwindle, forcing the castle garden wall to run straight into the sea. I can see why you'd buy this place: it's inaccessible in every sense. I gaze up at the windows

and nothing more than a feather floats down to us. It looks unoccupied.

"We'll have to go back," I say. "Find a way up the cliff."

"No, wait," says Sophia, pointing to a rough wooden door set into the wall. She tries the handle and it opens. She pushes in and Ned follows, which leaves me standing outside feeling stupid and nervous. Eventually, I peer around the door. It's a walled garden, filled mostly with flowers, but at the end tall pyramids of runner beans flag up the possibility of food.

I stand inside the door, listening. Apart from bird song, I can't hear a thing, not even the sea, not even Ned and Sophia's footsteps. Ned points at the runner beans and we creep deeper into the garden until we reach the vegetables.

Riches. Fat yellow carrots bulge out of the soil, long tresses of beans hang from the pyramids and wild strawberries dance along the paths. I cram unripe strawberries in my mouth before pulling a few carrots from a line; Ned picks beans and Sophia raises her eyebrows at us until I point to a lettuce that she wrenches from the ground.

I pull another — a snail sticks to my hand.

"Yuk!" I yell.

STUPID, STUPID, STUPID.

I hold my breath for about a minute.

"Flip," whispers Ned.

I swallow, ready to run, but no one comes so I pull up six beetroot and pick hard little apples from the tree growing against the wall. I turn to Ned. His backpack's overflowing, as are my stupid pockets.

"Time to go," I whisper, just a little too late, because standing in the entrance to the garden is a tall man with a pitchfork, and he definitely isn't a handsome prince.

Orange
----
squash

The inside of the castle is surprisingly modern. In fact, because of the small windows, rather than a view of the sea all anyone sees is smooth white walls.

We follow the silent man through silent corridors until we reach a door marked: *Estate Manager.* The silent man opens the door and nods for us to enter. Another man sits behind a desk, writing something in careful red capitals.

My mouth goes dry, and I drag my feet on the way into the room. It feels like real life has kicked in; I'm desperately tired but don't feel very hungry any more. Ned goes first, then Sophia, then me.

Sophia slips me a smile and grabs my hand. I try to smile back, but I'm too scared.

"I hate being in trouble," I whisper.

"Why'd you run away then?" mutters Ned, as if getting caught was my fault and shoves me towards a chair opposite the man with the red pen who appears to be the most miserable person in the universe.

The man's sunburned face is too long and the hairs that grow out of his ears are too thick. He's forgotten how to smile or even how to look up; either that or the paperwork on his desk is more interesting than we are. His lips move, so I lean forward to hear what he says.

"Kids today. Don't know the difference between right and wrong," he mutters.

I shuffle my feet. Behind the silent man who brought us up here is a fireplace with six carved wooden animals. They're too big for the mantelpiece.

"Shockin'." I look back at the miserable man, waiting for more, but he stacks the papers on the left of the desk, then picks them up again and moves them to the right.

We sit in silence.

This is like the chapter in *Castle of Doom* where the heroine is tied to a chair over a fire pit. There seems to be no possible way that she can get out of it.

There seems to be no possible way that we can get out of here.

I stare at my trainers. They're all earthy and I see that we've left footprints all over the floor. "Sorry about the mud on the carpet," I say.

He looks at me as if I've just landed from Mars, moves the stack of paper from one side of the desk to the other again and starts rummaging in a drawer.

I shrug and look at Sophia; she shrugs and looks at Ned.

We wait. I could do with using the loo but I'm too scared to ask.

A woman comes in with a tray of overly sweet orange squash and some Lincoln biscuits. She puts a cup of coffee in front of the estate manager, nods at the silent man in the corner, and slips out.

I nibble a biscuit, making it last, but I barely breathe.

We wait.

I look up at the silent man. He's got a drip on

the end of his nose.

The phone rings. The estate manager picks it up before it's even sounded properly and barks at it. "Yes… Yes… No… I won't." He slams the phone down and rearranges the desk again. It occurs to me that he's as uncomfortable as we are, but I'm still too scared to ask him if I can use the loo.

"This is Lostham Castle," he says suddenly. "It belongs to the Chief Constable who, incidentally, is on his way. You're the missing nippers from Bream?"

At this point, I notice that Ned has eaten all the biscuits.

"We are," says Sophia, slightly too loudly. "But it's not their—"

The man waves his hands at her as if none of it is his business, which I suppose it isn't.

He rises from the desk, unfolds himself and goes to the door. "I hate to lock you in like prisoners, but I'm going to – for your own good. Take those veggies out of your pockets and put 'em on my desk. I'll be back soon as the police arrive."

And he goes.

The silent man follows, rubbing his nose with a

grey handkerchief.

I wait a moment before trying the door. "We are locked in," I say.

"Flip," says Ned. He pulls Pinky and Perky out of his bag and slips them the beetroot leaves.

Sophia goes over to the window and opens it. "Too far to jump," she says. "I guess this is the end of the journey." She looks like she's going to cry. "But thanks so much for trying. Both of you." She closes the window and drinks the last drops of squash from her glass.

"If this was *The Prison on the Rock*, Sarah-Anne Wilmslow would have a rope in her bag..." I look up at Sophia; she's staring at me as if I'm mad. "But it's not, and we haven't," I finish, feeling foolish. "Actually, forget I said that. It was silly..."

"Well," says Ned, rummaging in his backpack. "For once, you might be right." And he pulls out a bundle of nylon that I recognise as a chunk of Mum's climbing rope, then throws an orange harness thing to the floor.

"What?" says Sophia. "Where did you get that?"

"Had it all the time," says Ned cheerfully. "After you ran away I put it in my bag, just in case."

A pain of intense regret washes through me. Why didn't I carry a climbing rope? Why couldn't I have thought of this? Sarah-Anne Wilmslow, where are you now?

"Well, we don't *all* have to get away, someone needs to stay at the top, just in case, but if Sophia can, that's the main thing." Ned finds the middle of the rope, loops it over his shoulder and around his waist before anchoring it around the leg of the desk. "This means there's a sliding rope and a holding rope and even if I get dragged across the floor, the desk won't fit through the window frame," he says in explanation.

Sophia looks doubtfully at him. "Am I supposed to climb down without a helmet or anything?"

Ned nods. "You have done climbing before? Haven't you?"

"Of course," she says. "Loads of times, but never without a helmet." She takes a deep breath and grabs the harness. She climbs into it, fits it around her waist and then clips one half of the sliding rope through it. She throws the holding rope out of the window. She tests the harness. "This is not how it's meant to be," she says, looking out to the sand below. "But..." She shrugs.

"Ready?" asks Ned, as I help her up on to the windowsill. "Here, you'd better take my bag with all the vegetables — I'm not sure..." He glances across at me.

"Not sure of what?" I ask.

"Which one of us will go with her," he mutters. "We'll talk about it."

"Thanks, both of you," Sophia says, leaning back on the ropes until Ned's feet slide the last inch and wedge against the wall. "You've been great."

And she disappears.

Abandoned

- - - - - - - - - - - - - - - - - - - -

I watch Sophia bounce lightly down the wall and unhook herself at the bottom. She clips the harness back on to the rope and waves up at us. All I can hear are seagulls. It's as if they're laughing at my attempt at having a proper friend.

"So," says Ned. "Who's going with her? We can't leave her on her own, she's clueless. But then, so are you – you haven't the faintest idea about survival."

"Hang on," I say. "We were supposed to be a team, and yet you'd leave me to face the police and Pinhead and everyone."

"I was simply thinking of the best way of saving

Sophia." He pulls the ropes slowly back through the window.

I breathe in but there are so many words to come out I can't choose which one's going first. "Saving Sophia?" I explode. "I'm supposed to be doing that! Right from the beginning you've just muscled in with your sad SAS stuff and your survivalist equipment and things. All that guff about sleeping under trees and tracks and hens. If it had been up to me—"

"You could have said."

I turn to the empty room, as if the chairs might back me up. "I *did* say, I said a million times, but OH NO, clever Ned, he's been listening to Mum and Dad, he knows exactly what to do, when his silly 'Eeeew' sister doesn't; he can take charge, he can be a hero."

"Right, you've made your point," says Ned, holding up his hand. "You go – you can look after Sophia. I can see I'm not wanted – time for me to drop out."

I stand, my mouth hanging open as Ned undoes the harness and holds it out towards me. "I'll keep them off you for a bit. Bye, sis – enjoy the rest of your trip."

And he pulls the rope around his back again and braces himself, gazing out of the window, every bit the selfless hero.

What?

I hold the harness in my hands. He's right, I haven't a clue how it works.

He looks at the wall as if it's really interesting. The complete toe-rag.

Buying time, I go back to the middle of the room and drink the remains of the orange squash.

I look out of the window. Sand at the bottom, but the bottom's still a long way away.

No, this is not how it's supposed to be.

This is unfair.

I did not think it would end this way.

Suddenly I have become a hopeless heroine. Not the strong decisive type but the bewildered abandoned type.

"Go on, then," says Ned. "She'll have vanished by the time you get down there."

I pick up the harness and tighten it around my waist and my bum, like Sophia did. Then I realise I'm supposed to have used the little metal clasp as well.

I hold the clasp, and the sliding rope, and I

114

wonder just how you're supposed to join them together. This is stupid.

I catch Ned watching me, but the moment I look at him he turns his head back towards the wall.

I drop the rope I'm supposed to hold on to out of the window. I look down its length. It's very long, very straight and very slidey.

When I get home after all this I'm going to kill him. Him, his snails, his stick insects, his entire collection of *EYE SPY* books, all of it, and I'll lock him in the boot of the car and make him listen to the sound of his possessions being destroyed, just like Dan Harper had to in *My Day of Revenge.*

I stand up, walk to the window and lift up my leg, and stop. I don't think I can do this.

This is real; this is not a story.

The shock of the revelation is so great that I have to sit down.

Ned's staring at me.

"Shall I go?" he says.

"No, I'm going to do it."

"But you don't know how, do you?"

I try really hard not to shout at him. "It's just this bit." I hold out the clasp.

He doesn't make eye contact. He swoops down,

tightens the harness, clips it to the rope and resumes his rope-holding stance.

"Ha," he says to the wall.

I recognise it as a "Ha" of satisfaction.

He knows I'm terrified, he knows I don't want to hang over a beach on a piece of nylon. I don't feel safe and I don't like feeling unsafe, but I badly want to be a hero, and heroes don't lie around worrying, they just get on with it. Irene Challis walked across Scotland, she didn't let a little thing like a small drop on a rope stop her from getting back.

I look out of the window again. I reckon it's not very far. If I fell, I'd only break my leg.

Wouldn't I?

I tie a knot in the holding rope about four feet from the top. It's not a very big knot so I take one of the African figurines from the miserable man's mantelpiece and tie that into it, like a toggle. I do the same thing again, about a foot down. I keep doing it until I've used up all six of the figurines.

"Sorry, animals," I say, tying the last knot. "But this is an emergency." They might not help much, but they'll give me more to hang on to.

I drop the rope back out of the window, and sit on the sill. It's further up than the floor and there's a breeze. I wasn't expecting a breeze.

I crouch – it feels better that way – and wrap the rope over my shoulder, across my back and under my arm until I've got a wooden zebra wedged in my armpit. It holds me and it doesn't seem to want to drop me, but I don't know what to do with my legs. I pay out a little more of the rope and walk down the wall about a foot. I probably couldn't climb back in through the window now if I tried, which means I can only go down.

Ned's face appears at the window above me. "That's it," he says. "You're halfway there. Keep going."

I look up at him. Something flickers through my fury – it might be guilt, it might be love – but hanging off a piece of string over a beach I can't be sure, and I can't spare the time to analyse it.

The stone grates on my knees. This is all real. The stone in front of my nose is real. The rope slipping slightly through my white fingers is real. My heart's beating as fast as I've ever felt it. Is this good? Would I rather be at home? Would I rather be with Miss Sackbutt?

I don't know – I can't work out if it's all just too scary or if I like it.

I take a deep breath and let the zebra go until I'm gripping a lion. The stone goes past in front of my nose and I graze my knuckles but I don't think there's much I can do about that. "Yay!" I say aloud, as cheerfully as possible, and slip down until I've got the giraffe in my hand. It's the last animal.

I look down.

Looking down is always a mistake and this is no exception. What I hadn't realised is that by tying knots in the rope, I was making it shorter. So now it's run out.

I look down again. I suppose it's only about six feet.

"Let go, sis," calls Ned. "It's not very far, you won't break anything."

A siren sounds behind the castle.

My heartbeat steps up a notch until I can barely hear the sea – I'm going to explode if I don't do something soon.

Above me is impossible. Below me might be painful. I hang for probably slightly too long before letting go.

Finding
Sophia

The sand is harder than it looks, and for a moment, I'm winded. I stand, bent double, gulping the air and waiting for my heart to slow down.

I'm alive.

I start to feel more normal and look around. I'm too obvious standing here so I run to the shadow of the cliff, glancing back to see if there's anything I can do to cover my tracks. Not really. Ned's taken the rope back up into the room but my feet have left perfect prints, and although Sophia's are lighter, even the dimmest policeman would spot them straight away. Short of a herd of elephants galloping through there's not much hope of hiding them.

I follow her faint footprints until they stop. There isn't an actual footpath, just a place where you might be able to scrabble up through collapsed stones to the grassy piece at the top. It's steep and I'm instantly out of breath, but I keep feeling that a policeman's about to jump up behind me, so even though I think I'm going to die, I manage to stumble over the crumbly sandy grass and out of sight of the castle. I find myself in a small clearing among tall thin pine trees. There's no sign of anyone.

"Sophia," I call, and my voice disappears into the thick pine needle carpet. Even my footprints don't make a sound.

"Sophia?" I wander through the trees following what must be a badger track. Sometimes I think I catch sight of Sophia's green shirt, but then it disappears and turns out to be a tree trunk. I can't hear the sea any more, just birdsong. It's like a green cathedral.

"Sophia?" Perhaps I should have waited at the castle.

I stumble on further and come to a timber yard. There are men working in the distance and several

120

pickup trucks parked at the back. To get past I'm either going to have to scramble through a mass of brambles or creep through the yard. The yard seems the better option. For a moment, I wonder if I could just walk through like there's nothing wrong, but then I realise that everyone must know about us, so I drop to my knees and crawl slowly to the pickup trucks.

I hover for an age at the back of the first truck, listening. The more I listen, the odder it sounds because although the noise of the chainsaws rings through the woods, I'm sure I can hear someone rustling, close by, in a whispery sort of a way.

"Sophia?" I call.

A yellow pile of leaves in the corner of the yard quivers and an arm pokes out. "Come inside," she says. "It's cosy."

"Are you mad?" I whisper, poking at the pile with my foot. "Two seconds with a sniffer dog and they'd have you. Come on, the police must be at the castle, I heard the sirens; we have to get out of here."

The pile of leaves shakes and Sophia emerges, grubbier than before.

"I couldn't think where else to hide," she says,

following me out of the yard and down the track, shedding leaves as she runs.

"Well, it was a rubbish idea." I stumble up to the left, through a thicket of bracken to the edge of the woods above the track.

"Sorry — I just thought it would be safer than standing there, waiting — where's Ned?"

I ignore her question. "They always have dogs. In books, they have loads, especially with missing children."

"Oh," she says. "And Ned?"

"Ned? He's being an idiot. He's not coming."

"Are you sure?" she says. "Don't you think we should wait?"

"I don't know," I say, a huge Ned-less cavern opening up inside me.

Dog
breath

We do wait. For about ten minutes. Sophia looks anxious and picks at her fingernails. I try to pretend I don't care, but actually I don't just feel sick, I feel as if my whole stomach's missing.

I don't understand it. I mean, I can't stand Ned, we're definitely better off without him, so why do I feel punched now that we've left him behind?

"We should get moving," says Sophia quietly. "You're right, Pinhead's probably got extra dogs in – Rottweilers or something."

"Rottweilers?" I say.

"With big teeth," says Sophia. "And heavies."

"D'you mean thugs?"

Sophia nods. The more I hear about Pinhead the more I can understand why she'd want to run away.

With every step that takes us back towards the castle car park, I'm expecting to be caught. In fact, I don't think I've breathed in for about twenty minutes. Not properly.

The tall yew hedge that encircles the entrance is all that's left between us and certain failure – or a faint chance of success.

"That's Wesson's, that black one, over there." Sophia crouches next to me and points at an enormous four-wheel drive with blacked-out windows, parked next to a couple of police cars. "Do you think this'll work?" she asks.

"I don't know, but I can't think of another way out of here."

We wait until the car park's silent. Distantly, I can hear calling and dogs, but nothing close up.

"Here goes," I say and step forward, out of the hedge.

No one shouts. No one moves to stop us. We stand at the back of the giant car.

Sophia opens the boot, and with my heart

somewhere near my heels, I follow her inside. The car's so big that we fit easily, there's enough room for us to lie under the black floor lining, and poke our heads along the edge under the shelf although there's no way of seeing if we're actually invisible.

"This is mad," I say.

"It's warm," says Sophia. "And comfy. And there are no sea creatures."

"I'm trying to think of a story where the hero has to hide in the villain's car, but apart from *Deadlock at Deadfall*, I can't think of any, and that one ends badly because the car goes over the cliff with the hero in it. He survives, but he has to swim the river and fight off a bear and he loses a finger and his girlfriend."

"Hmm," says Sophia.

Something crunches on the gravel outside, and I listen.

Wesson?

I imagine her opening the door and throwing her boots in. They'll be tall leather boots with spurs. On top of that she'll have a floor-length black leather coat, and golf clubs or a shotgun.

Or will she look first? Will she wonder what the

lumps are under the floor mat? Will she poke the end of the shotgun under the edge and lift it up so that we're caught like woodlice under a log?

Oh no – did the lights come on? I didn't notice. Will we be starkly lit by searchlights lining the side of the boot? Or is there some kind of alarm that'll tell her we're in here? Perhaps she already knows.

And how are we going to get out?

"Pinhead might be with her," whispers Sophia.

"What? I thought he was in New York."

Sophia doesn't say anything, just lets out a long sigh, followed by a tiny hiccupy sob.

"Sophia?" I whisper.

She sniffs. "It'll never work."

"It will," I say. "Ned will have told them something good." I manage to say it as if I mean it, but I'm wondering where he is. Is he even still at the castle, or is he on his way back to Bream?

Sophia laughs and sobs at the same time.

CLICK.

The driver's door?

But that's the only sound.

I daren't breathe, but if I don't breathe soon I'll choke. I let a little air out and suck a little in.

The car is utterly quiet. It hasn't moved – surely if she'd climbed in it would have moved? Of course, Sophia might be wrong and it might not be Wesson's car; it could belong to the miserable vegetable bloke.

Now someone's opening the boot. I lie completely still. If Wesson finds me I'm dead – I mean, I'll play dead and pretend I died in her boot; equally, I will die of shock. I'll have a Miss Sackbutt moment. But then it could be him – it could be the butcher, bouncer, racehorse trainer. Murderer? Pinhead. He might be bunging his golf clubs in.

"Just thought I'd check," comes a man's voice. "Oh, and does the dog go in there?"

Dog? What dog? Then I remember: Wesson's stupid terrier.

Something thumps on to the mat over my chest and every scrap of air I ever had explodes from my lungs.

"All right, boy," says a man's voice. It's definitely not Pinhead's, maybe it belongs to a policeman? The door slams shut.

It takes the dog a millisecond to find us under the mat.

It takes him two milliseconds to start licking my face.

The car joggles as Wesson climbs into the driver's seat, then shakes as the engine starts.

I close my eyes, screwing up my mouth so that my lips are sealed. Not even an amoeba could get through.

And suddenly we're moving, reversing, at speed and then thumping forwards through the lanes. The dog rearranges his legs but goes on licking.

The car revs as it takes the small hill up from the castle, and I imagine we must be passing the sawmill, but Wesson doesn't slow down and we swing on for about ten minutes.

The dog stops licking my face and starts licking my neck instead.

"Ugh," I cough. I breathe in thick damp dog air and wonder how long I can stand this for. As well as dog there's a strong smell of trainer. It's probably mine. I can't blame it on Ned any more. The hole in my stomach opens up again and I imagine him back in that room in the tower, this time handcuffed to the chair with no orange squash.

The radio comes on. It's a music station that I can't quite hear. Then the phone beeps.

I wipe dog spit from my face with the raggedy sweatshirt and strain to listen, but there's a great deal of expensive upholstery between us.

"No... The little horrors, they got away. I know, I know..." It goes quiet, she's still talking but I can't hear the words properly. "...jumped out of the tower!" There's more chat, but I can only pick up the odd word. And then she says: "I'll be back at Bream in an hour or so!"

There's a pause and she says. "Love you." And makes a kissing sound.

"Bream?" says Sophia, shaking her head away from the dog that is really fairly lovely as things with sharp teeth go but far too friendly when you're trapped under a rug. "But we want her to take us to Pinhead's office!"

"I think I heard her say Bream," I whisper.

The car pulls out on to a smooth straight road and picks up speed. "But we don't want to go back – do we?" I ask.

The dog curls up on my legs and settles its head on Sophia, gazing at her with big brown eyes. Perhaps it sees her as another potential lollipop.

"We've had it now," says Sophia. "She's going to drive us back and there's nothing we can do."

"I think we should get out," I say.

"How?" says Sophia. "We're going at sixty miles an hour."

"We need to make her stop," I say.

Tarmac

"We need to feed something under the back seat, poke her with it. That'll attract her attention. She stops the car; we run. In *The Dark is a Lonely Place*, Simon Strange uses a ship's flare to distract the helicopter pilot for long enough to jump out."

"He jumps – from a helicopter?" says Sophia.

"He's a very experienced sky diver," I reply.

"But we're not in a helicopter, we're in a speeding four-by-four – skydiving wouldn't really help us," says Sophia. "And we don't have a flare."

"Whatever," I say. "It worked for him."

Sophia falls silent. I can practically hear her thoughts squeezing out through her ears.

The dog rolls over so that Sophia can scratch his tummy. "Pinhead really will kill me if I keep this going much longer," she says. Her voice sounds worried.

"Would he actually?" I ask.

She looks across at me. "He wouldn't hesitate — honestly."

"But if we went back to Bream right now — we wouldn't really have caused any problems — would we? We could do that, you know — it might be the best thing."

"Lottie, he's nasty — he really is, I know I said he killed someone, well it might have been more than one — his brother went missing a year or so ago…"

"His brother?" I ask, pushing the dog's nose out of my face.

"Yes — he used to have a brother, they fell out and … the brother disappeared."

"How d'you mean — disappeared?" I say.

"He vanished. Pinhead just stopped talking about him — just as if he never existed. I think he might be dead."

"How – dead?" I ask.

"Under the motorway extension in West London, dead."

I feel as if another of those buckets of icy water has been emptied over my head. "Wearing a concrete overcoat?"

Sophia nods.

Mary Thirsk loses her husband to a concrete overcoat in the first chapter of *Death by Technology*. That's why she ends up pursuing the Mexican gun runners all the way to Berlin.

I do not want to go the same way, so I look around the back of the car for anything that might possibly help.

Sophia pulls herself out from under the dog and passes me a roll of green garden wire. "Found this in Ned's bag. Any good?"

"Brilliant." Feeling terrified, but not wanting to show it, I unroll the wire and poke it through the underneath of the back seat. I can just see Wesson's elbow. "Are you ready if I manage to get her to stop the car?"

Sophia nods.

I could try sticking it through Wesson's seat but there's always the chance that the wire'll get hooked up in the springs, so instead, I jab her elbow. Nothing happens the first time, so I jab it again and pull the wire back.

"Ow!" yelps Wesson, and rubs her elbow, but keeps driving.

I wait about half a minute and jab again.

"OW!" and this time she pulls the car violently to the side and slows down.

"Now!" I hiss at Sophia, who pulls the boot-release catch and disappears from sight. As the car almost stops, I jump too, taking the wire with me.

THUNK.

I hit tarmac and it hurts, but I realise there's only a split second before the car comes to a stop and Wesson gets out.

I scramble to my knees, but the dog's right with me, standing barking on the tarmac.

"Stay! Good dog, stay dog," I yell, leaping the crash barrier and stumbling down the embankment at the side of the road into a filthy stream. I look back to see if the dog comes too, but miraculously he doesn't. While I'm still staring, Sophia pushes my head down until I'm an inch from the fetid water and we lurk in a ditch with two beer cans and a dead badger.

The dog stands at the top and barks.

CLUNK. The door? Or the boot?

"Stupid animal, come on, back in." Wesson's voice.

She takes a minute to shut the boot.

CLUNK.

I hear Sophia's feet splashing behind me but I daren't look up to see if Wesson's worked out that there's a connection between the boot opening and being poked in the elbow.

We creep into a large drain that runs under the road and make silent whoops, slapping each other on the back and kicking the wet leaves into the air before realising that we never actually heard the engine start.

Which way's
----
north?

We stay down there for hours. Well, not hours, probably about twenty minutes, waiting for Wesson to find us. I know that if she appears all we'll be able to do is run in the opposite direction.

I'm thinking that although we didn't see one in the car, Wesson's probably got a gun.

She's probably going to shoot us, and leave us here in this drainage ditch.

I'm braced to see her at any moment.

A robin lands at the end of the tunnel, examines us, and takes off again.

A few minutes later he reappears, hops further

into the tunnel, takes a microscopic bug and hops off.

Perhaps Wesson's car's really quiet. Perhaps we wouldn't hear it start from here.

I realise that my heart has slowed to normal, that I've stopped sweating, that I'm breathing again, and that I've stopped feeling like I'm about to be murdered.

Murdered? I think about Pinhead leaning back against the kitchen counter and not drinking my dad's gooseberry champagne. He can't possibly actually be a murderer? Can he?

Sophia rustles behind me.

I glance down. She's examining the contents of Ned's bag again. "I just thought I'd check and see if Ned had a map or anything."

"Did he?"

She shakes her head. "Would this help?" she says, handing me the SAS survival guide.

I shrug. "He didn't leave the watch-compass thing by any chance?"

"He had it on his wrist, I saw him with it. But he left us the snails." She holds up the clear plastic box. The shapes of the two snails are quite clear inside.

"That's fantastic. Now we've got four mouths to feed, unless we let them go."

"We can't do that, can we?" says Sophia, clicking the lid off the box. "They're Ned's pets."

"They're also a food source," I say, flicking through the SAS guide, my eyes resting on the chapter title: *Get food where you can find it.* "We could eat them."

"You don't mean that," says Sophia. "Do you?"

I peer at Ned's snails; they have little grey antennae that seem to peer back. The fact that the snails are Ned's makes me want to eat them, but they look too curious and innocent, and anyway the only time we ate snails was with Dad and it was like eating elastic bands. "Maybe not. Look, this book's got a page about using the sun and moss on trees to find your direction. It says: *Moss grows on the north side of trees.*" I look around us in the tunnel. Everything's mossy, so everything in here is north.

"In *Long Afternoon of Death* there's a man who builds a compass out of a magnet and some iron filings."

"Have you got either?" says Sophia.

"I, um — no," I say.

She lets out a long sigh. "Thought not. Anyway, we can't stay here for ever, Lottie."

I try to think of a story with any other hints on direction-finding. I can't. There aren't any. I wonder how Irene made it across Scotland.

"Ok, we'll just have to read road signs."

Hours later, long after we've finished our water supplies, Sophia says: "I loved doing these sorts of things with my mum."

"Getting lost in the West Country?"

"No – adventures, out in the wild, no mobile phone, no car – just us and the elements." We clamber over a gate. "We trekked across Siberia one summer."

"Did you?" I ask. I thought Siberia was largely frozen, but I don't want to show my ignorance, so I say nothing.

"And we spent a few weeks in the Australian outback. Mum killed a snake and then we ate it."

"Fun," I say, surprised that Dad's never fed us snake and leading the way past some road works. A concrete lorry's dumping a load of soft concrete into a large hole.

"Sophia," I say. "When Pinhead's brother

disappeared, were they building the motorway? Only I thought it was built in the 1970s?"

There's a long silence, broken by distant dog barking. "Yes," she says quietly. "Or it might have been the new runway at Stansted airport."

"Oh," I say.

Seagulls

By the next day, we've stopped walking in straight lines. Instead we meander over open spaces peering into bins, searching behind food shops.

We're no better than seagulls.

In a children's playground, we find most of an abandoned picnic and a soggy bag of face paints.

Sophia crams the remains of a packet of salty biscuits into her mouth and hands me a net bag of tiny cheeses. I suck on a waxed cheese. I play around with it on my tongue. I make it last at least fifteen seconds.

Afterwards, I feel sick.

As we walk along footpaths, a haze appears before us. The large fields break down into smaller fields, and the lanes widen. Houses appear on the horizon, along with sheds, garages, trimmed hedges.

It's a town. Maybe a city, maybe it's Bristol, but as we haven't walked down a main road there's no way of telling.

I find myself looking for phone boxes. Ned's bag has the two fifty pence pieces that Dad gave us. I hope it's enough to make a phone call.

I imagine Mum and Dad sitting by the phone, waiting, the house quiet and empty without Ned and me yelling at each other, and I feel guilty.

At last, we round a corner behind a pub and I see a phone box.

But it doesn't take coins.

Nor does the next one, and the one after that's been turned into a book swap.

It is Bristol. But we must be miles out of the centre, because nothing looks like a city, it all looks like suburbs. We sit on a damp bench, shivering. I'm very hungry, very tired, and desperate for a bath, even in our bathroom where most of the time you have to flush the loo with a bucket. I expect Sophia feels the same. If I were able, I'd definitely ask Mum to come and get us, and risk being killed by Pinhead. It occurs to my sugar-starved brain that none of the heroes in Irene's books get hungry, and they don't seem to need sleep, either.

Although: "*In Footsteps to Timbuktu,* Anthea Sweetling is dying in the desert, and she does walk miles before begging food from the old woman in the village wash house," I say. "Hopefully we'll find something like that here somewhere."

Sophia sighs. "Do they have wash houses in Bristol?"

The back of my neck prickles first, and then my face as the blush spreads like ink across my skin. "Sorry," I mutter, mostly to myself.

We stumble on, cutting across the backs of gardens, scrambling through a newly scraped house plot, and emerging into an estate of yellow pretend-stone houses. Before long it becomes difficult to work out which way we've come from and which way we're going.

"But we've already walked down this road," I say, staring at a line of identical white plastic front doors. "Look, I'm sure we've passed that post box twice."

I sink down next to the post box. It's getting dark, and I watch as two crows fly to roost on a telephone line. Did Irene do this? Collapse on the edge of civilisation and watch birds going to sleep? Or did she tighten her brogues and keep marching?

A cat crosses the road.

I can't help thinking that Irene was tougher than I am.

I glance up the street, as Sophia sits down next to me. No sign of anyone else. Lights go on in the houses, a telly booms behind me.

The light fades really quickly and a street lamp comes on. It's lonelier here than it is in the middle of nowhere.

I'm feeling hungry and silly.

I thought my stories would provide answers – but they didn't. Not one of my heroes could give me realistic solutions and Sophia's obviously

unimpressed. The way she sighed when she asked if there were wash houses in Bristol!

Stupid.

Stupid stupid stupid.

I must look like such an idiot. But here's the most stupid thing of all: that I promised to help Sophia in the first place. That was *really* dim. And now we're here, in the middle of nowhere, with nothing to eat.

I scratch my back against the post box and shift my weight on the tarmac. I could fall asleep here. I think Sophia already has.

A fine drizzle starts to fall and I stick out my tongue hoping to catch a mouthful.

There's also the small matter of Pinhead and Wesson: a "murderer" and a mad woman with a dog, and probably a gun. When I think of it, no matter whether or not Pinhead's a murderer, Wesson's bound to have a gun. She's that kind of woman. She probably does the actual killing, with a tiny silver revolver she keeps in her iPod, before getting some thug to drop the victim into the concrete. Presumably, she doesn't even need a gun, she can just tie the victim's hands behind their back and shove them into the hole so that they slowly drown.

I imagine dropping into waist-deep wet concrete and adrenaline kicks in, waking me up completely and bringing on a dose of panicky breathing.

I should have stayed in the castle with Ned. We should have stayed together in fact, we should have all stayed in the castle, all met the Chief Constable, explained it all to Miss Sackbutt. This was never going to work. It wasn't the fact that there were three of us, just that the whole thing's faulty. We've got no proper plan, no proper proof. We've got a load of stories, some possible, some incredible. And I no longer know what to believe.

They all come from Sophia.

What do I know of her? Really, truthfully?

I can see she hasn't spoken to her mum in months. She gets emotional about that, so it must be true, and that's wrong. No one should be kept from their mother. I know that Wesson's after her, but then, Wesson would be after her whatever the background story was. All that stuff about dead people? It could be true. It could be rubbish. But then again – it might not be. A tiny part of me

trembles with excitement; the rest trembles with fear. And I think of Irene again.

Just then, it starts to rain in earnest.

No more
heroes

We spend that night in a bus shelter under Ned's silver-foil survival blanket. It's raining hard now and I know that I'm cold. Sophia must be freezing; she's got bare legs. We huddle together, sharing a tomato and a piece of stale pitta bread with Pinky and Perky, collecting drinking water in a hollow made out of the corner of the survival blanket.

We gaze long and hard at Ned's egg, wrapped in his school sock safe in the mug. He'd curled it right round, so that the egg's in a grey nest.

"Oh – how sweet," says Sophia.

I try not to cry. It's only an egg. "They're very tough, egg shells," I reply, my voice slightly wobbly. "They're made of mostly grit – or calcium." I lay it back inside the sock nest. "Save it until we can cook it?"

Sophia nods, and nibbles another crumb of pitta.

A man walks past with a dog. He's texting and doesn't even look at us. I tense, as if I might run and get his attention, but Sophia's talking again.

"Tell me a story, Lottie – tell me one of your book stories."

"Really?" And I risk it. "I thought you thought they were stupid."

"I never said that, it's just—"

"What?"

"It's just that they're not very helpful when we're trying to do something."

"Like climb out of a window?"

"Yeah – like that. If you think about it, they're just not very realistic, are they? I mean, I know Ned had a rope in his bag, but the chances of that were a million to one. Just because one of the characters in a book had a rope in her bag doesn't mean you're suddenly going to have one." She looks up at me. "Does it?"

"No – I don't suppose it does."

"What I mean is, they're just stories – they're escapism, not real life."

I think about how to say it. "But your life is like the stories," I say. "Larger than ordinary life. Almost incredible."

Sophia nods her head and takes a long time to answer. "Yes it is, but it's not all cut and dried like it is in books and films. My life is – messy. I can't explain." She looks out into the rain.

"Tell me about the good bits, tell me about your mum," I say.

"Mum? Well, she's an actress."

"Actress? I thought she was a singer?"

"Yeah, a bit of both, musical comedy, opera – that sort of thing."

"I see."

"And she laughs a lot, has blonde hair, blue eyes, plays the piano – she used to have fans and fan letters, and then she started to buzz around the world, and I went, too."

"So when did you live in the flat over the tube station?"

"Oh – that, yes." Sophia coughs and throws her plait back over her shoulder. "That was in between

150

times, when she was resting."

"Oh – I see."

"It was wonderful but it's all in the past now. But hopefully we can find the office tomorrow, find out where she is; catch her before she leaves the UK. We need to press on."

"Tonight?"

"Tomorrow will do," says Sophia. "I'm pretty sure she's here till Tuesday."

I wonder how, without knowing her mother's stage name, Sophia can be so sure of it. But I'm too tired and I let it pass.

We sit in silence while two cars whizz past, splashing through puddles and soaking the bus shelter. A few drops fall on the survival blanket and trickle down, yellow under the streetlight.

"I could tell you about a real life hero, if you like," I say.

"Yes?"

"There was this woman – she was called Irene, she lived in the house up the road from us…"

Ewoks

The centre of the city comes as a surprise. We walk over a bridge above a river and into some quiet streets of houses, but within minutes we're surrounded by people, hundreds of them doing their Saturday shopping. Rushing back and forth. We stand there looking damp and mad, with a pound and two Roman snails between us and destitution.

Sophia shelters in a doorway and I follow. We watch the families with shopping and food, and proper clothes.

"We need to find Pinhead's office, then we can

break in and find out where Mum is."

I would now eat paving stones if I could work out how to cook them. Everything is clouded by a desire for food, but on the streets there's nothing to eat but cardboard and pigeons.

I think about Irene, walking across Scotland and wonder what she ate to keep going. Birds' eggs? Mud? Moss? Any of them are probably more nutritious than cardboard.

We drink water from the tap in the public toilets, emerging into a crowd of people dressed as teddy bears.

"What's going on?" Sophia asks, shivering outside the toilets.

Behind the teddies, a Princess Leia and two people in Star Trek uniforms duck into the loos.

I stare after them.

"Oh, I get it. They're Ewoks," says Sophia.

"What?" I ask.

"Ewoks. From *Star Wars*. That's what they're dressed as. It must be a carnival thing."

Watching them moving, I realise that I can hardly see the people underneath the clothes. "We could find the office in disguise and creep in under cover of sci fi," I suggest.

Sophia widens her eyes. "Are you serious?"

"Yes. In—" But I stop myself. "I'm sure people do that kind of thing all the time."

"In what book are there aliens in PE kits?" she says.

I kick the pavement. "Have you got a better suggestion?"

By some giant wheelie bins, we find a carton of cardboard tubes and a length of green carpet. Also a load of used but only slightly cheesy tinfoil, ten rock-hard croissants and a packet of pink paper cups. We eat the croissants and tear holes in the cardboard tubes so that the paper cups stick through them. Covered with tinfoil they look like a two-year-old's vision of a submachine gun.

"They'll do," says Sophia, pretending to shoot the wall.

I pick up my gun. I've never felt so self-conscious, but once we step out into the hordes of badly dressed aliens, no one even glances at us.

A lorry grinds slowly through the middle of the crowd with a band on the top playing something

loud but oddly muffled. They shed short lengths of silver cloth that I rescue and drape around my neck.

From another lorry, a silver hat frisbees into the crowd. I scoop it up and jam it on to Sophia's head. A little further on, we gain a papery skirt, a plastic sword, and a breastplate. We're starting to look the part.

"This way," says Sophia, drifting to the right of the main street.

Tall brick buildings rise from the pavement, their windows blacked out. As our fellow aliens wander through the streets, the huge windows of the office blocks gleam with their shattered reflections.

Security guards loll in the doorways, pointing and laughing at the costumes.

"Excuse me." Sophia walks up to one of them. "Any chance we could use your loo?" She hops from foot to foot.

The man scratches his head. "Um – don't see why not," he says and shouts back into the darkness of the building. "Here, Steve, can these kids use the toilets?"

"Sure," comes the reply.

Sophia pulls my arm and, confused, I follow.

And then I understand.

On the wall is a list of the people who use the offices.

Pinehead Associates appears to be on level three.

"You'll have to take the lift," says Steve, who turns out to be a slack-jawed tapeworm staring at a screen dotted with footballers. "I could show you, but I'm watching—"

"S'OK," says Sophia breezily. "Where do we go?"

"Any of the floors, they've all got toilets. If you like, you can both go to different ones." His eyes never move from the TV. I glance back at the doorway. Security guard number one's still glued to the aliens outside.

"Perfect," I say, as we head towards the lift. "Do you think they recognised you?"

Sophia pauses and shakes her head. "No – no – I don't think so – do you?" I look back at the security guards. Neither of them seem to be paying us any attention. "What's the plan?" I whisper.

"We'll break in, see what we can find," says Sophia. "But perhaps we should keep the lift going up and down, we could pretend we've gone to different toilets on different floors like he said.

Let's make them think we're playing in the lift."

I follow her in, see her press 3 and do my best to keep reality at bay. "OK," I say. "Fine — it's a plan."

The third
----
floor

The third floor is exactly what I expected. Pot plants, air conditioning, weird padded silence from a white thickly carpeted floor. For a millisecond, I feel jealous; I'd like that carpet, those leatherette chairs, but it occurs to me that no one who works in the building has ever kept chickens or potted up cuttings or made their own hedgerow jelly, and I experience a slight sense of superiority as if I've glimpsed another dimension that they don't even know exists.

Sophia stops outside a glass booth. On the door it says *T. R. Pinehead*.

She turns the handle.

The door's locked. Of course it's locked, but above it is a keypad. "Any ideas?" I ask.

Sophia sighs. "Date of birth? Mine, his, Mum's?" She taps at the keys. "Random numbers?"

"Favourite songs?" I ask. "All one number? Actually – let's have a look at that." I peer at the pad. The seven and the eight are both worn and grubby with use – all the others are pristine and shiny. I try 8787, then 7878, then 7887, then 7788 and the door clicks open.

Sophia looks at me. "Clever," she says, pushing open the door.

"We'll have to be quick, though," I say, following her inside. "That football match was in the second half. He'll notice if we're not back by full time."

Standing here, in the office, I feel utterly terrified. This is not the kind of thing I'm meant to do. I do not do breaking and entering. I do top-quality English Comprehension and play the flute. I do not sneak around reading other people's secrets, especially not scary people.

I try to forget that what I'm doing is illegal and dangerous. Instead, I look around.

It's all very white and squishy, lots of leatherette

and deep pile carpet, and more silence. A single white computer sits on an enormous desk that is otherwise utterly blank.

"Where do we start? What are we looking for?" I ask.

"Here," says Sophia, moving towards an old green filing cabinet, standing by itself and looking out of place in this smooth new office space. "I've seen him lock it after he's put things in it. We might find his address book or diary."

"Are you sure?" I open a long rolling cupboard door to reveal ranks of white filing cabinets, all unlocked.

"Yup," she says, opening a desk drawer. "It's just that we need the key."

"Or a screwdriver – that's what they always use…" I say. Sophia glances up at me. "Well, they do. Even Dad uses one when he can't open things."

I find a pair of large scissors in a box underneath the desk and try slipping the blade into the lock. It doesn't work – it's obviously the wrong thing to use.

"Bingo," says Sophia, holding up a tiny key.

But we've bent the lock, so even with the key it takes ages to get the drawer to open.

160

And when it does, I don't understand what we've found.

"What are these?" I ask, flicking through ledgers filled with hundreds of tightly written numbers.

Sophia shrugs. "Or these?" she says, pointing at a collection of flash-drives and camera storage discs. "We should take them," she decides.

"We need to copy them," I say.

She stares at me.

"Otherwise it's inadmissable evidence."

She still stares at me.

"If you take them, you can't prove they came from here, but if you copy them, then they won't even know you've seen them. If it ever comes to a police investigation, then the police have to find them here otherwise they can't use them as evidence."

"Let me guess. You know that because it's in something like *The History of the Swollen Shrew?* Or *Dark Days in Kansas?*"

"No. This time I heard it on the radio." I smile.

"OK, I get it," says Sophia. She reaches into another drawer and pulls out a brand new, unopened flash drive. "They always have stacks of these."

She switches on the white computer, and copies the disc files from the individual chips to the new flash drive, while I begin to scan the ledger into the photocopier.

"What about his diary — should I be looking for it?" I ask.

"I'll check his engagements on this." She starts to click through Pinhead's emails on the computer.

I'm so intent on the photocopying, I don't see what Sophia's doing, and don't look up until I hear her make a little choking sound.

"What is it?" I ask.

"Nothing — we have to go." The screen on the computer fades into black.

I scoop the copied pages from the printer, and turn the ledger over to get the last few entries.

"I'm done," she says. "Do you want to do the lift thing? Or shall I?"

"Nearly finished," I say. "We could do it together."

We pick up every scrap of tinfoil, I stuff the photocopied diaries into Ned's bag, and we try to put the filing cabinet lock in the right position.

"Right," says Sophia, putting the key on the window sill. "Time to get out of here."

But we don't have time, because the lift pings. We stare at each other. Sophia pushes the office door shut and runs for the big white cupboard of filing cabinets. I stuff the cardboard guns into the broom cupboard and dive for cover under the kneehole of the huge desk that is too small and too public.

I hear the peeping of the keypad outside. The door handle clunks and someone comes in. I draw my knees into my chest and barely breathe.

"So do you think it was them?" It's Wesson's voice.

"Bound to be." Someone tries the drawer of the green filing cabinet. I hold my breath but it stays closed. "Haven't got in here, though, have they, so what's she playing at?" A man's voice. Pinhead.

Something sounds like it's being dragged across the carpet. I really hope we haven't left anything out there.

Knees appear right by my head. Pinstripe-suited ones. Then very close by, I hear the high-pitched beeps of someone putting numbers into a phone. Pinhead starts talking.

"Yeah, it's me. Yes, we're on the trail. The security boys downstairs rang me." Silence while he listens for a bit. "Yeah, Sophia, and the other girl – they're somewhere in the building." He listens. "Look," his voice softens, like he's just flipped the charm switch. "Don't worry – they won't be able to stop us, we're nearly there." More silence. "Yeah, yeah – I've got it covered – there won't be any loose ends. You know me, I never leave loose ends."

If I had to run, I couldn't. My foot's fallen asleep.

There's a sound of sticky tape coming off a dispenser.

"Look – it's fine – it's all safe, no one knows anything – no one even knows about this phone. There's nothing leading from me to you, nothing leading from the warehouse to me. No one knows anything. It all looks kosher."

A pause. And I think about how different he sounds. Not at all like the man that was charming Miss Sackbutt in our kitchen.

"Yeah – yeah. Anyway, it's just a blip, they're just children, tiny schmucky children. Don't worry about it. I'll take care of them – no problem."

The phone clunks on to the desk above my head. I look up instinctively, and to my amazement see a huge bundle of cash taped to the underneath of the desk. I draw myself away from it.

"What did Jim say?" asks Wesson.

"Wants to keep his nose clean – worried about

164

his public reputation."

A different phone beeps. A call in or out? "Yeah? No, I don't *actually know.*" Pinhead's voice is different, more irritated than in the last call. "Yes – yes – don't worry, I'll find her." Fingers drum on the desk above my head. "No – I said I would, OK? Yes, I lost her but I'll find her. Don't panic and don't hassle me – I'm doing my best OK?"

The phone clunks back on to the desk.

"And?" says Wesson.

Pinhead's talking: "She's antsy, she's worried about her little darling – but it'll be all right. OK, let's find those kids, and this time, if I catch that toe-rag Sophia – I swear I'll kill her." His hand reaches under the top of the desk, towards the money.

I pull back. Instead of taking the cash, the hand holds a mobile phone under the counter top. With his other hand, he presses sticky tape to either side until the phone is stuck fast to the underside of the desk.

"Right – time for me to get out of here. You all right staying here, darling? Keep a look out and give me a ring if anything happens. I'll go and search the rest of the place."

"Of course, Trevor, love. Take care."

Then there's the long sticky sound of kissing.

Trapped

Pins and needles are worse the longer you leave them.

When Wesson helps herself from the water cooler, I risk moving my dead leg. It's excruciating. Absolutely agonising. It feels as if someone's pulling it off my body and it's all I can do to stop myself from screaming.

I think of Irene flying those aeroplanes, stuck in the same position for hours in a freezing cockpit. If she could do it, so can I.

Mind you, she didn't have Pinhead after her. Racehorse trainer, bouncer, boxer, sausage maker, international criminal. Gangster. Spy. Murderer.

All the stories of concrete overcoats and missing relatives become horribly possible. I keep playing the conversation over in my mind. *No loose ends. No loose ends.* Am I a loose end?

And who was the second caller – was it my mum? Or Miss Sackbutt? Maybe Sophia's mum – though it sounds like she's already propping up a motorway in Japan.

Away to my left in the cupboard of filing cabinets, Sophia has managed to stay completely silent, but I'm wondering how long I can stand this for.

Are we going to have to wait for Wesson to give up and go home?

I watch the sun cross from one side of the room to the other, the lights come on in the office, and finally, I listen to the sound of Miss Wesson bedding down on the floor, her head scarily close to my ankle on the other side of the backboard of the desk.

For some time Wesson's breathing's fast, too fast to be asleep, and then it turns from fast to slow, and I wonder whether I could sneak out past her nose, but I'm not at all sure I could walk well enough.

De dee dee, da dee dee, da da dee dee dee.

A mobile phone rings and I use the noise to shuffle my legs while Wesson gropes to switch it on.

"Yeah?" she says.

Silence.

"Oh."

Silence.

"Well, you've got the car but I could get a cab, meet you there."

Silence.

"See you in half an hour and, Trevor, love you."

The carpet crunches as Wesson stands up and fabric rustles. She pulls on some sort of clothing, and then there's an empty silence as the door clicks shut.

I sit motionless, waiting.

Ping.

The lift doors clunk.

The whole office floor feels wrapped in cotton-wool silence. I risk pushing my leg out of the side of the desk. No one leaps on me, no one shouts, although everything aches.

I stand, my legs shaking and pull back the door on the filing cabinets.

"Lottie?"

At first I can't see her, then I realise she's crammed herself into the gap along the top but so far back that only her eyes give her away.

"She's gone," I say, reaching my hand out to pull Sophia from the space.

It takes a few minutes to get her out, and like me, she's seized up.

"Did you get that?" I say. "The conversations?"

Sophia nods. She gazes at me, wide eyed. "See – I said he was scary."

I wipe a homesick tear away from my eye. *I'd really like to go home now. I want it all to stop.* But instead I say, "There's a bundle of money under here. And a mobile phone."

Sophia drops to her knees and peers under the desk.

"There's loads. Hundreds. What did he mean, Sophia – about the loose ends?" I say, swallowing the tears, trying to sound sensible.

She pulls out the bundle. It's a thick wad of twenties wrapped with a paper band and a bank stamp. "I don't know, Lottie." She shivers. "Do you think it would be wrong to take this?"

I stare at the bundle, and think of the

conversation we just heard.

"No, I don't. Take the phone, too, and let's get out of here."

149 steps

It's easier to think about leaving the office than to leave it.

"They'll find us in seconds if we use the lift, we'll have to go by the stairs," I say.

"Do you think they're still looking for us?" Sophia says, pulling open the heavy fire door.

"I do. They never saw us leave. They must still think we might be here," I say. "Up or down?"

"Why up?" she says.

"They'll expect us to come out of the bottom, so perhaps we should try the top."

We start climbing the stairs. I lose count after

six floors, in fact I can't even work out which way I'm facing. I realise that I'm much more at home in the countryside, where I can see the sky. Here, without the sun, there's nothing to tell you where anything is.

I'm boiling within seconds, and out of breath within minutes.

"Do you think Ned told them we were coming here?" she asks.

I walk up another flight of steps. Would he or wouldn't he?

An improbable thought comes to me. "I suppose he might have been worried about us?" As I say it I feel something curious, that's not just to do with being out of breath. A kind of warm, sweet sadness, that comes with the thought of my brother actually caring about me.

I push it to one side and make myself walk up another flight of steps. Sophia skips up the last few steps and I rush to follow.

A minute later and I'm regretting it. These buildings are seriously tall. So tall that you can hear them blowing in the wind, and the tops are not nearly as smart as the entrances would make you think.

I would rather stamp up the staircase forever than be stuck here on top for one minute.

We step out into a howling gale. Rain beats on the roof all around us and it's freezing. I stop in the doorway, letting my eyes sort the shapes in the dark. Tall chimneys thrust up into the rain cloud, aerials, pipes, all standing dark against the yellow nightglow of the city. Things I can't see scrunch under my trainers. Gravel? Seagull bones? Eggs? Poo?

Sophia picks her way through the shafts and pipes to the side of the roof. I can see her clearly now; it's not at all dark really. A steel parapet runs around the side, with one small gap.

"The fire escape?" she shouts.

I lean against the wind. I can barely walk on the flat so how on earth am I supposed to go down a fire escape? This was mad – I should never have suggested it.

Sophia leans on the parapet, looking down. "It's not too bad," she says. "A ladder for a couple of storeys then a proper staircase."

"Really?" I say, as my ladder dream comes back. I can't move.

"If you don't look down, Lottie, you ought to

174

be able to climb it." Sophia stands, her feet already below roof level, and beckons to me.

This is not good. This is exactly the kind of thing that stopped me from wanting to go to Bream Lodge and they've got a safety net there.

I walk towards her, keeping my eyes on her eyes and avoiding the huge falling landscape view behind her.

"Turn around, Lottie."

I turn.

"Get on your hands and knees."

I drop to the ground. Fragments of concrete and roofing felt dig into my palms. This could be the last time I ever look at anything close up. A tiny snail clings to the side of the parapet. How did he get all the way up here?

"Now put your feet down on to the first rung."

I stretch my leg down, feel the step in the arch of my foot, and pull the other leg down, too. I'm shaking. My whole body is shaking. I am not designed to do this.

"Put one hand on either side."

I grip the black handrail. It's rough, badly painted, slightly rusty – exactly like the ones in my dreams although this one seems quite solid.

The roof, the last solid thing, disappears upwards in front of my nose.

One step, two step, three step, pause.

The ladder just goes down and down.

One step, two step, three step, pause.

One step, two step, three step, pause.

Sophia talks to me the whole way, calling encouragement.

"Nearly there, Lottie!" she shouts. "You're doing so well."

I'm doing well. Yes, I have to remember that; I'm getting there, even with the gale whipping around my head and Ned's backpack pulling me towards the ground.

Ned. If he were here he'd be doing this; he'd even be enjoying it.

I wonder what happened when we left him. I've never even considered what he might have felt as I jumped out of that window or that he might actually have enjoyed the adventure. He would have loved this. A pang of guilt flashes in my brain and for a moment I'm almost not scared, just conscience-stricken.

I stop, and look down. Between me and where I think the ground is, I can see a criss-cross of bars;

they might be close, they might be miles away, but they move over the lights below when I move my head.

Moving my head. Not a good idea. I go back to staring at the wall in front of me and put my foot down again.

I must do this. Irene walked across Scotland. Flew aeroplanes on her own. Worked as a doctor in war zones. She was real, not just a character in a book. She really did it.

One step, two step, three step, pause.

One step, two step, three step, pause.

"One more, Lottie!" yells Sophia, and my foot grates on a wider piece of metal.

"This is the fire staircase," she says, her hand on my back as my legs fold. "You absolutely can't fall off here."

"Really?" I say, although I don't think Sophia can hear me — the wind's doing its best to steal my words.

The wall in front is still concrete, but just at the level of my feet it changes to glass. I sag to the metal platform and wait for my heart to steady.

Sophia talks right into my ear. "Ready for the next bit?"

I suppose I'd hoped we could just stay here, but I half stand, although my legs feel soft and unreal. She turns and I follow her down a metal staircase that seems to go on forever.

We start slowly, but I begin to get into a new rhythm and Sophia speeds up.

One two three four five six seven, turn, three paces, one two three four five six...

I lose count, but the ground comes up to meet us, and soon cars are whizzing by underneath, and street lights glow warm and welcoming. We're probably still three storeys up, but it feels like we're reaching the ground.

Sophia stops. There are lights on in the windows at the bottom level.

"They won't see us," I say. "Not if we stick to the outside of the staircases."

We run the last six sets of stairs, and then there's a tiny ladder that I race down before following Sophia into the darkness at the end of the alley.

Fluffy bath
robes

The Japanese receptionist covers her surprise when Sophia counts a pile of twenty-pound notes on to the counter.

"And," Sophia says, as if she's done this a hundred times before, "could someone go out and get us some clothes? I imagine there must be a supermarket somewhere that's open. Size four shoes for me."

"Oh, and mine are five and a half," I say, as carelessly as I can.

We head for the lift, catching a disapproving glance from a middle-aged couple arriving at the hotel with expensive luggage.

In silence, we head for the fifth floor, open the door to room 507 and throw ourselves on to the bed.

"Whoa," says Sophia.

I'm actually too tired to say anything at all.

She bathes first, while I try to ring home.

There's no answer and no way of leaving a message. They're either out looking for us, haven't heard we're missing or they're feeding the chickens.

I lay the phone back in the cradle. I feel horribly homesick.

Ned must be home by now. Miss Sackbutt must be back. I imagine all of them at home, worrying about us. I try the number again, but there's still no reply and I just make myself miserable by imagining the phone ringing in an empty kitchen, all the plants listening to it sounding in the darkness. The old black phone ringing quietly next to Mum and Dad's iron bedstead. The office phone, buried under piles of paperwork and newspaper cuttings. I imagine the rain beating on the windows, and the hens sheltering under the coop.

I reach into Ned's bag. My fingers rest on a

book and I pull it out. It's not the SAS survival guide. It's *The Severed Foot.* I open the cover. There's Irene's name, but inside there are signs of Mum among the pages. Leaves and scraps of the parish magazine used as bookmarks, tickets from the National Humus Society Museum.

I hold a dried hornbeam leaf against my face and think about Mum.

Although I thought I never would, I miss her, and I'm beginning to think I might have got her wrong. That she doesn't just like nature and science, that maybe she craves something else, like I do. Perhaps that's why they go moth-hunting without a phone, alone in the elements? Perhaps she, or maybe she and Dad, need excitement in their lives. Perhaps what goes on inside Mum's head isn't at all like the person she seems on the outside.

And what about Irene? Did she crave excitement? Is that why she had all those books for when she was too old to have any more adventures?

"Your turn," says Sophia, throwing herself on the bed trussed in white towels. I stuff the book back in the bag, but leave the hornbeam leaf on my pillow.

For the first time in nearly a week, I enter a bathroom.

It's the bathroom of my dreams. White, sparkling, loaded with fluffy towels, glittering with mirrors and downlighters. A shelf of small plastic bottles under the mirror. Shampoo, conditioner, shower gel, all the things I've ever dreamed of.

Heaven.

But it isn't home.

I bet when I flush the loo, it doesn't make the pipes sing.

I bet there aren't woodlice under the bath.

I turn on the shower. Sophia has left it on exactly the right temperature.

Delicious. But I can't enjoy it.

Hot water, gallons of it, pours from the showerhead and I look down by my feet to see the week of twigs and mud and sweat sweep in a river down the plughole. *This should all be happening to Ned,* I think.

The water beats on the top of my head, scouring my scalp, turning my skin red.

I imagine Ned rolling on the floor next door, hooting with laughter about our escape from the rooftops. He'd have loved it. He'd have been good

182

at it. And this, the posh hotel with all the shiny stuff, all paid for with Pinhead's money. He would have loved the idea of that.

I think back to the moment in the miserable man's office.

I squeeze a huge dollop of shampoo on to my hand.

I wish we hadn't fallen out.

I stay in the shower for so long, the effort to leave it seems too much. If the hot water could go on for ever I'd sleep here.

Sophia is dressed in badly fitting jeans and a sweatshirt. Somebody's been to the shops and bought us a selection of nasty clothes.

I struggle with some trousers, but settle on a black skirt, black tights, trainers and a hoody. The hoody has "Princess" embroidered across the chest and down the arms in purple sequins but I don't honestly care, I'm just glad to leave the tracksuit behind. I brush the tangles from my hair and use the glittery hairbands provided to jam it all into a bun.

"Fourteen, maybe fifteen?" says Sophia.

"What?" I say, peering at myself in the mirror. I

look like a stranger.

"How old you look. And tell me, what do you fancy from the menu? I'll call room service."

We order burgers and chips with ice cream and chocolate fudge cake to follow.

"So where's your mum?" I ask. "Did you find out?"

"I did." Sophia grabs the remote control, flicking over to a film.

"And?" I say.

"And she's performing in London."

"London?" My stomach lurches.

"We could catch the train. Would you mind?"

I would mind but I don't say it. "Of course, we'll go tomorrow. So she's not dead then?"

Sophia shakes her head, staring at the screen.

"We could watch the news," I suggest, "see if they're still looking for us."

She shakes her head. "I really like this film – can we watch it?"

I sit and stare at the telly. It's an unlovable film about a dog. I don't care about the dog or its owner, and I'm slightly cross about not being able to watch the news. I don't say anything, though.

Instead I flick through the mobile phone we took

from underneath Pinhead's desk. It's got loads of numbers, times of calls. But none of the numbers are labelled "dodgy bloke" or "hired gun".

I press the red button and the screen goes dead. I sit staring at the dog on the telly.

Knock knock.

I freeze.

"Room service," says a man's voice.

This is the bit where the hired assassin comes in and shoots us.

But it's just a man with a trolley. A trolley heaped with chips and burgers and salad and iced tea. A trolley of complete bliss.

And guilt.

I take Pinky and Perky to the bathroom, wash out their box, and give them two large pale lettuce leaves.

At least they got to stay in a hotel. I'll take them back to Ned, like a souvenir. If we ever make it home.

Escape

My dreams are filled with images of Mum and Dad setting off on an expedition. Ned's with them and they all look really excited, but I can't hear any of them, I can't hear the words, I can just see their lips moving. They reach out to me, and I reach out to them, but Pinhead and Miss Sackbutt stand between us, waving golf clubs, and Sophia's way off to the side, singing loudly and dancing with a tennis racquet.

I pull at Mum's hands but they shrink from mine, until she's nothing more than a tiny speck, vanishing into the dark.

186

I wake before light, trying to work out where I am. Sophia is fast asleep. But something has woken me.

I look outside the window. It's raining, but there's a police car parked down by the entrance to the building opposite.

Poo.

"Sophia." I nudge her awake. "We need to go. Now."

"What?" She's still asleep.

"Now — let's get out of here."

I stuff the remains of last night's food into Ned's bag along with the spare clothes.

Sophia slides off the bed and on to her feet. She leaves two twenty-pound notes on the side, stuffing the rest of the bundle into her jeans.

I open the door, fully expecting to find a policeman out there, but the corridor's empty. We tiptoe away from the lift towards the stairs at the end of the passage. Everything is utterly silent.

The fire door to the stairs is heavy, so I hold it for Sophia, and pull hard so that it barely thumps back into place. Sophia points down, but I point up.

- - - - -

"Not the roof again?" She opens her sleepy eyes wide.

I shake my head and set off up the stairs. My legs complain; yesterday was the worst of all the days we've had so far and I could have stayed asleep forever.

We climb two flights, our feet tip-tapping on the steps, our breath far too noisy. I pull open the fire door on to the seventh floor. Silence. We tiptoe past a tray of dirty crockery left outside a bedroom door; instinctively I check it for leftovers but it's just crusts, nothing worth having, and we go on until we reach the lift.

It's clanging somewhere down the shaft. Doors opening? Closing? Sophia shrugs and presses the call button. We stand outside the doors before ducking out of the way seconds before the lift arrives. It stops and the doors open. I creep back until I can see inside. It's empty.

"Quick, Sophia."

We stand inside the lift, looking at the buttons.

"If we go to the bottom, we have to go through reception to get out," she says.

"If we go to the basement, we probably have to go through the kitchens or something."

188

We choose the first floor and step out into another silent corridor. At the end is the staircase again, so we take it and tiptoe downstairs. A glass window in the door allows us to look through into the lobby. It seems deserted. I push open the door. It's still absolutely quiet.

Our feet don't sound on the thick carpeting, and there's this soft tinkly music in the background that muffles everything anyway.

Sophia heads towards the main entrance. I follow, holding my breath, expecting the police to jump on us at any moment.

The door opens quietly as we approach. Looking back, I see a man in reception, his back to us, shuffling through post, drinking coffee.

"Bye," whispers Sophia and we creep out into the street.

"Sophia and Charlotte."

I look up from the shiny black shoes.

Pinhead.

And he looks furious.

I turn to run, but he grabs me by the elbow. Sophia makes it a few metres down the road only to be stopped by Wesson, who leaps from a parked car and sprints after her.

"Right, tie them up," says Pinhead, gripping my arm so tight that it hurts. "Here – to the car." I'm dragged over the pavement, pulled by my elbow, until my arm reaches the bar of the front passenger seat headrest.

"Help!" I shout, my voice sharp across the empty streets. A flock of pigeons jump into the air and Pinhead laughs, but nothing else happens.

No one runs to help us.

"No one around, see. Good timing, by the way. We thought we'd have to get you later on, pick you out of the crowds – but you made it easy." From his pocket, Pinhead takes a bundle of small black plastic things. I recognise them as cable ties; Dad uses them to hold the car together. Pinhead tightens three around my wrist and loops another three through the front headrest chaining me half-in, half-out of the back seat of the giant car. Seconds later and Sophia joins me, her hand looped to the door handle on the other side.

"You two have caused me a lot of trouble. But you're not as clever as you think, are you?"

I stare at the carpet. I don't want to look up at

him, see the satisfaction on his face.

It doesn't seem to bother him. He keeps talking. "I don't know how you got hold of the phone, but it made you easy to find." I look up and he taps his nose. "Smart phone, see – not a stupid phone. Right, let's get moving."

Stupid.

Stupid stupid stupid.

"Get in," says Wesson, a faint sheen of sweat on her top lip. She pushes me up on to the seat and shuts the door. Pinhead slams the other side and clambers into the front, locking all the doors. We're trapped. No one can see in; the car's tinted windows see to that, although it's irrelevant, there's still no one around at this time in the morning. I look back towards the hotel. The doors are closed. It looks asleep.

Across the road, the police car seems deserted.

Poo.

I got it all wrong.

Fear

- - - - - - - - - - - - - - - - - -

We drive out of town along a fast and empty road. I'm so scared that I can't make myself breathe properly. I'm panting, but feel as if I might explode from lack of oxygen. Compared to this, climbing off the roof of the office building was a picnic. This is like a gangster movie – except it's real.

After a few minutes, the dog sticks its nose over the back seat.

"Hello, dog," I whisper.

He responds by licking my neck and panting in my ear.

"Buster!" shouts Wesson. "Down."

The dog slinks back. If I turn my head really hard I can just about see him. "Hello, Buster." I smile at the dog.

He smiles back.

"I'm really sorry about this," says Sophia under her breath.

For a nanosecond I feel like telling her life was boring but safe until I met her; now it's exciting but I've been kidnapped by a madman murderer and his moll. Instead I say: "It's OK, Sophia, I'm sure you'd do the same for me – let's just get through it."

My voice sounds really calm and ordinary, but I don't feel like that – I feel panicky and screamy and like leaping up in the air and leaving my spine behind.

But there's nothing I can do.

The road winds into woodland. Beech trees with a thick carpet of fallen leaves stretch away from us. It looks very lonely. It makes me think of the Gravelly sisters in *Body in the Waves.* They were fed poisonous mushrooms in the woods and then hidden in a wardrobe wrapped in gingham. But I don't say anything to Sophia. I glance across at her. She's gone white. The thing about the Gravelly sisters was that they left a crucial letter for Verity

Potsdam to find, which is how she discovers their bodies in the gingham wardrobe. I can't write a letter. Instead, I reach into the bag and fumble until I feel the flash-drive that Sophia used to copy the files.

I slip it into the palm of my hand. If I could throw it out of the car I would, but that's not going to work. I'll have to hide it where I am. It slips into the crack between the seats. It may never be found, but it's possible that it might in years to come be discovered by some mechanic, and then someone'll know. Someone'll know exactly why what happened to us happened. Whether they find the bodies or not...

Pinhead pulls into a layby next to a spewing rubbish bin. "OK then, time for a chat," he says, looking in his mirror.

Wesson turns around and glares at us over the back of the seat. "Let's have the phone for starters," she says. "What've you done with Trevor's phone?"

"In the bag," I say, nodding at Ned's bag lying on the seat between us. The phone's sticking out of the top.

"Pass it over," says Pinhead.

Sophia reaches into the bag and hands the phone

over the seat. "Here," she says quietly.

"And the money?" he says over his shoulder.

For a moment I think she's going to pretend that we never saw the money. But she rummages in her pocket and sprinkles a confetti of mangled bank notes over the seats. "There," she says.

"Thank you," says Pinhead. His voice is crisp with fury. He rescues the money and jams it in his jacket pocket. "And while we're about it, we'll have the bag – hand it over and Maria can check through it."

Sophia sighs and heaves the bag up on to the seat back. It's got all the photocopied entries from the diary. I catch her eye and try to smile, but she doesn't seem to see me.

I want to tell her that I've left a legacy, that the flash drive will survive us. That I've had a good idea from a book and actually carried it through. But she's not looking.

Wesson searches the bag and pulls out all the photocopies. "This is – this is what?" She waves the papers under Pinhead's nose.

Pinhead sits back, looking through the windscreen. "Give those here. Actually, I think you'd better search the girls, Maria. Check their pockets. I'll just take a look at the oil and the tyres."

Something crosses his face; a flicker of irritation that suggests that he didn't want her to know about the papers. And she looks worried, just for an instant. It's the first time I've seen them anything other than united.

He climbs out of the car, opens the boot, takes out a small tool box and crouches down by the front wheel. Things clunk against the side of the car and I hear the sound of a pressure gauge. Somehow I didn't have him down as the pressure-gauge type. I imagined he handed a car over to a garage or a hotel and got it back in perfect shape.

Perhaps he's avoiding her.

Maybe he likes her less than she likes him. In *Gold Under the Aspidistra*, Dana Scour gives up everything for Denzil Johnson who turns out to be a complete scoundrel. The only difference is that I like Dana Scour.

Wesson clambers in with us. Anchored as we are by the cable ties, there's no point in struggling. Although she looks as if she dislikes it as much as we do she enters into the squirmy business of searching us with her usual speed and efficiency. She starts with me, checking the pockets of my hoodie, my skirt, inside my shoes, and comes up with some chips and a load of hairbands. She's far too close, and she smells of aftershave, Pinhead's aftershave. After she's given up on me, she crawls across the back seat to Sophia, and I hold my breath as her hand rests briefly on the gap between the seats, but the flash drive must be nice and deep because she doesn't find it. Sophia pouts her mouth as if she's going to spit at Wesson; she doesn't.

Through the window I watch Pinhead take the papers to the verge. He pulls a lighter from his pocket and lights the corner of the first sheet. He burns each one, corner to corner, then stamps the ashes into the grass. Then he climbs back into the car.

Poo.

"Nix, nada," says Wesson, opening my door and going round to the front of the car.

"Thanks, darling." Pinhead leans across and plants a cold peck on her cheek.

Wesson turns and kisses him back. Properly. I glance at Sophia. She's turned to stare out of the window.

"Good," he says, starting the engine, and the car glides out of the layby. "Swap over at the station?"

he says to Wesson.

"Yeah." She looks at her mobile, and plugs it into the little stand by the radio. "You should make the 9.15. I'll take the cargo to the warehouse and meet up with the boys. Are you sure you'll be all right, Trevor?"

Pinhead stares straight ahead as we drive out of the woods and the view opens up towards the sea. A long way off, a squall scurries over the water, changing the silver to grey and back again.

"I'll be fine," he says. "Don't you worry. I'll sort it out at the other end – and I'll meet you on Wednesday.

"What about *her*?" says Wesson.

Again, Pinhead stays quiet. Eventually, he says, "Don't you worry – there's nothing to worry about. Everything's sorted."

Lottie Green: hero
Part I

We drop Pinhead at a set of traffic lights in a wet town.

He takes a small bag and waves goodbye to Wesson before diving into the railway station. He doesn't look back at us.

Wesson swings the car into a U-turn and we head out of town, slightly too fast.

"Where are we going?" Sophia asks.

"Never mind — you'll find out soon enough."

We seem to be going south, but I'm not sure any more. I'm not sure about *anything* any more. I hope this isn't really happening. I hope it's happening to someone else called Lottie Green in a book and that the fictional Lottie Green is going to be able to think of a way out of the situation.

But the doors are locked and my hand's attached to the seat in front of me. What can this Lottie Green do?

Wesson pulls on to the motorway and we turn north again.

Irene must have felt this way when she was flying through the fog: no idea where she was or where she was going, but prepared for any eventuality. Perhaps she too looked to books for inspiration. Perhaps she too looked to the story of Richard Standfast in *Calm Before the Storm* for hope and guidance, remembering how he crash-landed his plane in the desert sands just as she thumped hers down on to a Scottish hillside.

We pass lorries and vans and cars, Wesson driving faster than I would imagine was safe, and then at the next exit, she pulls off the motorway again. The car leaps as she slams her foot on the brake and then the accelerator. It throws me across my seat, from left to right and back again.

I brace myself for the next bend but it arrives too soon, shooting Ned's bag along the seat and

on to the floor.

The dog whimpers and tries to stand.

Wesson hunches closer to the steering wheel as she wrenches it from one side to the other.

It's a very big, very powerful car, and it slows and speeds on this little road impressively. I can't help feeling that she's only just in control of it.

The phone rings and, taking one hand from the steering wheel, Wesson grabs it. "Hello, love. Yes. I've got that," she says.

There's a train, a long intercity train crossing underneath us.

"Can you see us? We're crossing the bridge now," says Wesson. "You're near the front? I can't see you." She peers out over the bridge, concentrating more on the train than the road. "And you will be there? As arranged?"

The car swings out and back, narrowly missing a cyclist, and only just making it round a big bend in the road. The train runs parallel with us and I look across to see if I can see Pinhead. I somehow doubt he'd wave at us, but Wesson might wave at him. Her one hand is white on the steering wheel, the other still holding the phone, and I can see that every muscle in her back is tense. "…my swimsuit's packed. I'm missing you already."

This is not good.

The train's gliding through trees, splitting away from us. And it's faster than we are.

"I can still see you," says Wesson.

I bring my knees up in front of me and slip my bum down so that I'm curled up and can't really see out of the window. I wish I could bring my hand close and wrap myself in my arms, but it's still tethered to the back of the front seat.

"Love you, miss you – can't wait." Wesson makes a long sucky kissing sound. "Bye," she says, looking at the phone.

"Sophia," I say. But I don't get any further because the tyres judder and we're flung from one side to the other.

GREEEEEEAAAAAAAACH!

I whack into the window, my cheekbone striking the glass, but before I've even rubbed it, the world turns upside down.

GREEEEEEEAAAAAAAACH!

It all happens in slow motion – clothing flying across the car, a dog lead, a bar of chocolate – and the screech of metal.

GREEEEEEAAAAAAAACH!

The tyres squeal, someone screams, it could be Sophia. Glass explodes inwards from the windscreen, bushes bang against my side window then Sophia's window, then mine again and each time I feel as if my head's going to fall off. We settle upside down and my hand dangles underneath me, my legs apparently attached to the ceiling of the car thanks to the super-efficient seatbelts. Grass thumps over the roof, mud flies in where the windscreen should be. There's more tearing, screaming, revving.

And then silence.

Huge ordinary empty countryside silence.

Birdsong.

Rain falling on leaves.

The train horn sounding in the distance.

I move my head.

Below me, on the ceiling, the dog whimpers. He's standing on three paws, deep in the glass that must have been the windscreen. His eyes are wide and dark. He's holding the fourth leg up to me.

"S'OK, Buster," I say. But my voice wobbles; I can barely hold it together.

He wags his tail and licks the fourth paw. I can't see anything wrong but he's holding it like he's hurt.

"Sophia?" I ask, looking across. She's hanging in an awkward position, her body seems to have folded. "Sophia?" But she doesn't move.

Buster moans, and rolls over to lie on his side. My head feels as if it's going to explode. I really need to get myself the right way up.

I reach over and unclick my seatbelt that drops me down towards the ceiling of the car, crunching into the glass and just missing poor Buster. I give him a stroke and I crouch, rubbing my elbow where the cable ties still hold me to the seat back. "Don't worry, fella…" I start, but I can't speak properly. I can hear the fear in my voice.

I unclip Sophia's seatbelt and she slides to the ceiling, held upright by the cable tie joined to the door. She moans as she moves, so at least I know she's alive. There's no blood.

Wesson's another matter. She's crumpled. Her seatbelt has come undone and she's wrapped in the tatters of the air bag. She looks like she might be dead. I can't reach her because of the cable ties.

I listen, expecting the sound of sirens, but it's all quiet. The only noise is some distant crows. From my memory of the road, there was no one else around, although in the end, the cyclist would

catch up with us. Surely.

Something drips at the front of the car. Although I don't think it's petrol it still makes me feel nervous. I don't know much about cars, but I don't think anything that comes out of an engine is good for you. Now we're upside down, everything that normally relies on gravity to stay put must be free to escape.

I sniff the air. Now I *can* smell petrol. And I remember that above my head is an enormous petrol tank just waiting to leak all over us.

I swallow and try to think about Irene, in an aeroplane, crashed in the fog.

She did it.

So can I.

Lottie Green: hero
Part 2

I can't reach Wesson's mobile. It's clipped to a
stand in the front of the car about a foot further
than my arm goes.

"Excuse me – Miss Wesson!" I shout but she
doesn't answer, doesn't move. "Maria!"

Still no response.

I lean down to look out of the windows. It's
not easy to see anything because they're smeared
in mud. I expect the whole car's covered in the
stuff and it seems to be surrounded by brambles.
I try for the millionth time to pull my hand out
of the plastic tie, but I can't move it. Dad says

they're unbreakable.

I look around for anything that might let me reach the phone and my eyes fall on Buster. He's picking at his paw.

"Have you got a piece of glass in there?" I ask, scooping him up and holding the damaged foot. There's no blood, but I can see a fragment of the square windscreen glass caught between his toes. I flick at it with my fingernail and it pings out across the car.

"There – now let's see if you can stand." I drop him on to my legs and he tries all four feet before licking my chin and slobbering over my neck.

"Thanks, Buster. Now, do you think you could be useful and get me that mobile phone?"

He clambers off my leg and tiptoes through the glass to Sophia. She groans as he licks her hand.

"Buster?" she says feebly.

He pants and wags his tail.

"Sophia – are you all right?" I ask. She looks very uncomfortable, jammed against the door.

"I'm – OK – I think," she says. Her legs stretch out over the glass and she tries to pull her arm underneath her. "Ow – this hurts." Her ties, just like mine, have stayed firmly whole.

Buster wanders over to the front of the car. Using his mouth, he grabs Ned's bag and pulls it open, rummaging inside. He pulls back, Ned's survival blanket pinched delicately between his teeth.

"Brilliant, Buster. Great start – not a phone, but bring it here." He pads around to me, and wrapping the blanket around my hand, I sweep the glass to one side. I stroke his head and give him a cold chip from my pocket.

He chews on the chip and shuffles back to the front of the car. After a little rootling, he brings me an umbrella, followed by a glove, a road atlas, a pair of Ned's pants and a packet of mints.

"Can you smell petrol?" says Sophia, suddenly wide awake.

"I can," I say calmly, offering her a mint. "But I'm hoping Buster can help to get us out of here. Have another look, Buster, see what else you can bring me."

He brings me the other glove, Pinky and Perky in their box, the egg in a cup, and a car jack.

"Not a mobile, but that's still fantastic, Buster," I say, handing him another chip. I weigh the car jack in my hand. It's very heavy. It must be good for something. I swing it round and smash the rear

window. With my foot, I push out the remaining glass. Buster wriggles out, peers at the brambles and comes back in again. It doesn't do any good, just makes the smell of petrol stronger in the car.

I breathe slowly, and wonder whether petrol is less dangerous when it has more air. Probably not.

Buster smiles at me hopefully as if I might take him for a walk.

"What are we going to do, Lottie? The car'll blow up."

"Don't worry – we'll find a way out," I say.

Buster picks up his lead.

"I'd love to take you for a walk, Buster, but I'm stuck." My voice goes up at the end. I'm trying very hard not to cry, but it's going to happen soon, and then I know I won't be any use. I pull at my wrist and he wags his tail and stands on his hind legs. He picks up the car jack and hands it to me again.

I run my finger along the metal edge and rest it against the tie. It's rough, but not really sharp. I rub it back and forth pressing it against the plastic of the tie, but after five minutes the cable tie looks untouched while my wrist looks sore.

"It's not going to work, fella. I need some scissors or a knife."

"Pinhead has a penknife," says Sophia. Her voice trembles. "And he's on the train. Ned's got one too."

"Are you sure?" I glance at her, hopefully.

She shakes her head. "It's not in the bag. I checked, he must have had it on him when we left."

Buster yips and raises himself on to his back legs to lick the plastic ties. He bites at them, nibbling around my hand. His tooth catches but the plastic's too tight against my skin, and really tough. I'm sure he could chew through it eventually, but not soon enough. I pat his head and he drops back down.

"Thank you, Buster – but I don't think it'll do any good."

He nuzzles my leg. We sit listening to whatever it is that's dripping, the smell of petrol getting stronger.

I wonder how easy it was for Irene to get out of her crashed aircraft, aviation fuel all around her. She didn't give up; she made it out.

Sophia sobs, wiping her nose on her sleeve. "I'm sorry, Lottie, I am, I'm really sorry. I didn't realise how—"

"Don't worry – I'm going to get us out of here."

I really wish I could believe myself but I've got to be like Irene. I've got to behave like her. I mustn't give up.

I look again at the head rest. It has two long stainless steel posts that go into the seat. Perhaps it pulls out? I push as hard as I can; it doesn't move but it looks as if it ought to. And then I remember the car jack.

Wedging the car jack between the seat and the seat back, I try to turn the wheel on the end to make it open, but it's fiddly and it's really supposed to be done with a metal hook. I know; I've seen Mum do it on our car.

I look around. The umbrella has a hook – but it's too big.

"Hold this," I say to Sophia, handing her the umbrella. "Hold it really tight." Using Sophia as a clamp, I tug the large plastic hook from the skinny metal rod inside. It almost fits in the wheel at the end of the jack. I turn it, and the jack opens out, filling the space. Although the rod keeps on pinging out of the jack, after a few minutes I can see that the head rest is pulling away from the seat. I add my foot, jamming it into the space and try to stand on the head rest.

It slides to the ground, the cable ties slip off and I'm free.

"Whoa!" I say.

"Hey – brilliant!" says Sophia, and we stop, staring at her cable ties looped through the handle of the car door. Apart from removing the door, I don't see that I can get anywhere with freeing her.

"Right," I say, "just give me a moment. I'll think of something."

I scrabble over the glass and out of the back window. Buster comes with me, leaping and laughing and generally looking happy enough to explode.

We stand in the rain, breathing the fresh air.

"Thank you, Buster – you're a genius."

He picks up a twig and holds it in his mouth.

For a moment I want to burst into tears, but I swallow, trying to keep my mind focused on what I need to do. "Not now, Buster – in a minute."

I turn away from him and he scampers around to stand in front of me. "Sorry, fella." I step over him and go round to the front of the car. It isn't that easy because the brambles reach my knees, but luckily the car roof has mangled and flattened a large enough area to make it just possible. I tug

at Sophia's door, but it won't open, none of them will. It must be because the roof's too damaged. I try the driver's door.

It doesn't even move.

The smell of petrol is strongest at the front of the car, and it takes all my will power not to run away. Instead I turn and clamber back in through the back window, all the way through until I reach the front of the car.

"Have you had an idea?" asks Sophia.

When I open the glove compartment, a load of random things cascade to the ceiling. I search excitedly through the muddle, but there's nothing useful. Only water, tissues and maps. Nothing sharp.

"Do you think the window glass would cut it?" she asks.

Experimentally, I run my forefinger over a square of the broken glass. "It's safety glass," I say in the end. "It won't cut."

Sophia lets out a long trembling sigh. I can hear the sob just beneath the surface.

"If I can reach the mobile I'll ring for help," I say, not saying that the help had better arrive quickly before the car blows up.

Crunching over the ceiling, I get myself next to Wesson. I can't see where she's hurt – if she is hurt – but I can hear her breathing.

I unclip the phone from the stand, my fingers pause over the buttons. Something triggers a memory. "Petrol stations. Don't they have a sign about sparks and petrol and mobile phones?"

Sophia's eyes widen.

Holding the phone like it's a bomb, I slip backwards out of the car and, with Buster in tow, clamber up the bank behind us to stand on the side of the road.

Up here, I can't smell the petrol. I flick open the phone, and dial.

Death by

toast

The police station is over-warm and smells of disinfectant and wee.

They still haven't worked out who we are. Apparently the car's registered to a man in Dubai and they're trying to ring him. They've been trying to ring him ever since I showed them the car upside down in the ditch.

Buster and I sat at the top of the bank in the rain, waiting. It didn't take long for the firemen to arrive. The police were slower.

"Cuffed to the door?" said one of the firemen trying to get Sophia out of the car.

He snipped off the cable ties and pulled her out of the window. She sat breathless on the wet grass for about a second before she ran up the bank towards me.

Wesson was trickier; it took three firemen and they had to cut the bottom off and tip the whole car over. They'd sprayed everything with a white powder first, to stop the petrol exploding, so it was also very messy and undignified. I didn't really feel sorry for her, though.

Buster and I watched and the firemen gave us both some chocolate.

When the bottom of the car was back on its tyres, I asked a fireman to get Ned's bag, the egg and Pinky and Perky.

"Got your homework in there?" he asked, handing them over.

I smiled. "Sort of."

I didn't want Ned's bag, I just didn't want it to lie there rotting in the rain and the broken glass.

Apart from sore arms, there was nothing wrong with us, so we ended up in the back of the policeman's car, with a coronation chicken sandwich and a bag of Maltesers to share. We pulled away from the accident site, leaving firemen

and policemen measuring and filming and talking.

Now we're back at the station everyone seems to be full of ideas about how it happened, but they haven't asked us a single thing.

"She was abducting them—"

"Selling them overseas—"

"Excuse me," I say.

"She's obviously mad, and she must have been driving too fast—"

"Excuse me!" I shout.

A policewoman stops spreading butter on a piece of toast and puts her hand up. "Shh, everyone – listen."

I hold Buster's paw in my hand, to give me moral support. "I don't know if you're going to believe me..."

"Try us," says a policeman, using his handcuffs to get a tea bag out of a cup.

"She's called Maria Wesson, and she works for a man called Trevor Pinehead."

"Pinehead? Don't I know that name?"

"Kids – the kids who went missing down in Devon – that's you – she kidnapped you?"

Sophia nods, I shake my head. "Yes," she says.

"No," I say. "No – we..." I look around at them

all. Five policemen and one woman, all listening to me. "We did run away, from Bream Lodge."

"Sounds about right," says one of the policemen, rustling through a pile of old newspapers. "Here you are." He holds up a picture. It doesn't look very much like me. Sophia looks gorgeous.

"That's us – and we made it all the way to Bristol."

"Charlotte Green," says the policeman with the papers. "Right – Batson, go and look up the case, ring Exeter and get the number for the parents."

A young policeman races out of the room, clutching the paper.

"What were you doing in Bristol?" asks the policewoman.

The words hang in the air for a really long time, and I wonder whether to try and tell them the truth. They're listening, and there's never going to be a better opportunity. But Sophia kicks me, and whispers: "They're not going to believe you."

"It's her guardian – he's dangerous – he's a murderer," I say, my voice disappearing on the word *murderer*. "He's killed people – been to prison."

"Really?" says the policeman with the newspapers. "This same bloke here? He's rather sophis – I'm sure I'd have remembered that from the telly."

"He might not actually have been to prison," says Sophia. "But I'm sure he's killed people."

"Let me get this straight – you say your guardian is a murderer?"

"Yes – I mean – no – I mean – I don't know," says Sophia.

"Let's check," says the policewoman. She turns to a computer and taps in Pinhead's name. We all wait. The policemen cluster around the screen.

"Nothing. Nothing except for parking fines."

"But that can't be true," I say, turning to Sophia. "You said—"

"Well, I thought he was..." says Sophia. "I'm sure he's killed people, he might never have been caught, that's all."

"Hmmm," says the first policeman, looking up at me.

Sophia stares at the floor.

A dark cloud of doubt drifts into my mind. Then I remember the cable ties. "He cuffed us to the car," I say. "That's not normal, is it?"

The policewoman nods. "We'll be prosecuting the woman, but there's nothing to link her to Mr Pinehead at this stage."

"But he was there – he was the one that put the

cable ties on us. He caught us when we came out of the hotel," I say.

Sophia looks up. "It's true and he had a mobile phone with lots of telephone numbers, and a warehouse, and all sorts of things. And he's got loads of money from somewhere."

The policewoman tilts her head. "I understand what you're saying, but there's no proof. At the moment, Mr Pinehead is a very respectable figure."

"But he's not — you should have heard what he said on the phone," I say.

"Did you record it?"

"No." I pick up Buster and hold him on my lap. If they won't believe us, then I want them all to go away. And I want to talk to Sophia on her own — I want to find out the truth. And then I remember the flash drive.

"In the back of the car, in the gap between the seats, there's a computer storage drive thing — we copied everything from his office. I bet there's something on there — could you send someone to look?"

The policewoman brushes crumbs from her chin.

"I don't think it's going to help, do you?" she says.

"Please, there must be something. Otherwise why would he chain us to the car?"

"Because you keep running away?" says the policeman with the newspapers.

"We'll see," says the policewoman, in the same way Mum does when I ask for something that she's got no intention of letting me have.

Sophia picks dog hairs from her trousers.

I feel so many conflicting emotions that I can't decide what I'm thinking. I just know that I really badly want to go home, that I really miss my family, the food, the house, the crack in the ceiling.

Ned.

"What happened to Ned?" I ask, remembering him for the first time in ages.

"Ned?" says the policeman with the newspapers. "Who's Ned?"

"My brother?" I say, my lip wobbling. If they don't know, perhaps he didn't get home after all.

The policeman flicks through the papers. "Sorry — don't know anything about Ned."

I wipe a tear away with Buster's ear. He looks up at me and licks my face.

* * *

We sit there for hours. I take Buster out to wee on a police car and bring him back inside. We sit for even longer. The policemen concentrate on their toast and coffee, swapping Marmite for jam and back again. They seem to have forgotten us.

The phone rings and the policewoman answers. "Yes, sir — we'll get them to make a statement, yes, we're just waiting for family liaison or a relative. Oh, that's good to know, yes, I'll pass it on." The policewoman puts down the phone. "It seems Maria Wesson is conscious and willing to talk."

They all nod sagely as if a significant breakthrough has been reached.

"So that's good," the policewoman repeats brightly, handing me yet another piece of toast.

I'm just wondering what Maria Wesson will say, when there's a lot of noise from the corridor and Mum bursts in, her face tearstained and swollen. Behind her, Ned, also tearstained.

"Lottie," she says, wrapping me in her arms, my face enveloped by her old padded jacket that smells of guinea pigs. "Lottie. I thought we'd lost you."

The long
road back

"He's not our dog," says Mum after she comes out of the interview room. All the tears have gone now and she just looks utterly furious.

"But his owner's in hospital – can't we look after him?"

Mum turns and stares at me. "Lottie. After all you've put us through you expect me to house a stray dog?"

Sophia looks at the floor.

Ned bends down and rubs Buster's ears. "He's a nice dog."

"He saved my life," I say, and my voice goes

wobbly. "And Sophia's."

Mum goes tight-lipped and sweeps out of the police station. I pick up Buster and we follow.

We drive along what seem to be identical roads until we're on the motorway. Although I'd love to talk to Ned, I keep quiet – I know Mum too well. She grips the steering wheel and mutters to herself, periodically wiping her nose on her sleeve.

Ned's in the front seat. He turns to me. "I've got something I ought to tell you – I found out—"

"Ned," says Mum. "Not now."

"But, it's—"

"I don't care," says Mum.

Ned reaches for the radio button.

"Don't!" snaps Mum. "I'd rather drive in silence."

Ned sighs.

I sigh, too. I want to know how Ned got home. *When* he got home. Did Miss Sackbutt tell him off or feed him KitKats, or both? And when did Mum and Dad find out we were missing? I'd also like to tell Ned about the flash drive, and the car crash and climbing over the glass, and I'd like to tell Mum about Irene, how Irene kept me going, and the books, Irene's books – our books. But I don't

do any of those things; instead I lean against the window, my hand on Buster's head, watching the wet countryside. I glance across to Sophia. She's sitting still, her eyes closed, tears racing down her cheeks.

We screech into the drive and tumble from the car into the house. It's tipping with rain, the garden rustles and gurgles as Dad's clever water retrieval system rescues every drop that falls, sending it into a giant underground tank which then pumps it out to the loos as faintly green water for flushing. I've always thought it was stupid, but now I'm not so sure.

It's better than trying to catch drinking water in a scrap of tinfoil from a survival blanket.

Dad's there, waiting just inside the door; he's made toast and scones, and searched out a jar of his really quite edible hedgerow jelly. He grabs me and drags me towards him. Then he spots Sophia and hugs her, too.

"Sweets, darlings… I—" But he can't speak, any more than I can. His beard tickles against the top of my head and for the first time in days, I feel safe, completely safe.

Mum, on the other hand, has thrown the car keys on to the table and stands with her arms crossed. She's wearing the biggest scowl I've ever seen. She is not happy.

"And...?" she says, looking from me to Sophia and then back to me.

"Mum," starts Ned. "This is all—"

"We didn't mean for it—" I try, but Sophia's faster and louder. I sink into a chair and butter a scone while she speaks.

"It wasn't Lottie's fault, or Ned's. I kidnapped Lottie, she was in the same kayak as me, and then I forced her to come with me and then she had to come, and then Ned found us and I forced both of them to come with me..." Sophia's voice fades.

Dad stares at her. Mum stares at her. "Yes?" says Mum.

Sophia takes a deep breath. "I kidnapped them, I steered the boat so Lottie couldn't stop us, and then I ran when Wesson came, and they came too, and I made it so that they felt they couldn't leave me, but—"

"Wait a second," says Dad, pouring Mum a coffee. "I don't think we need to know how. I think

it's more a question of why."

We're silenced.

Dad sits at the table across from Sophia and looks at her with his most serious face, the one he keeps for plants. "Why, Sophia, did you feel you had to run away?"

Sophia bites her lip and looks across at me.

"Because of Pinhead," she says. "Because he's stolen my mother, my everything. He knows where she is, but he keeps it from me, he's up to something, he's not..."

Sophia trails off. Mum's shaking her head.

"It's not true, is it?" she says. "It's not true that you never see your mum — that Trevor Pinehead took her away — is it?" She doesn't say it aggressively, but the words seem to take the stiffening out of Sophia's back, and she wilts. Mum goes on, so quietly that I can hardly hear. "I mean, yes, your mum is mostly abroad, but, Sophia, where does the truth begin and the story end?"

There's a knock at the door. Dad goes and we sit silently around the table, listening. It's a woman's voice, one I don't recognise.

A long slow tear escapes from the corner of Sophia's eye and creeps to the corner of her mouth.

"What's going on?" I say, standing, scone in hand.

Dad ushers a tall dark-haired woman into the room. She's Sophia in twenty-five years' time. She has Sophia's dark eyes, dark hair, dark skin.

She smiles, a broad, white-toothed smile. "Sophia," she says, her accent southern European, the word springing from her tongue. "Mrs Green emailed me, I came as soon as I could—"

Sophia leans over and buries her head in her hands.

"Who…?" I ask, gazing at this woman. "Are you Sophia's mum?"

Dad takes off his glasses and rubs them with the corner of his T-shirt. He sighs and shakes his head.

The woman slides into a chair next to Sophia. She appears weightless, fragile, deeply sad. She puts her hand on Sophia's shoulder. "It's me, Sophia my love. Tell me, what has been happening?"

I look towards Ned. He's pink, like he might explode. I can almost hear his brain. "Yes – this is Sophia's mum. We found her."

"You?" I gasp at Ned. "How?"

He turns to me. "I looked her up on the internet. Mum and I did – in the library – we found her

name, found her email and sent her a message. It seemed sensible."

I sit with my mouth open.

Sophia has a mum. A very beautiful mum, a very elegant mum, but a mum all the same. One who doesn't seem all that dead or distant, one that seems to be able to turn up and find her daughter.

One with email.

Ned tries again. "Sophia told us a story, didn't you? It was a good story, but..."

Sophia bends her head and uses her hands to cradle her face. When she looks up, she's tear-sodden, her long black eyelashes heavy with crying, her eyes bloodshot. "I – Oh, Lottie!"

"What? What's going on?" My head fills with yellow and black and red and chaos, and I'm confused.

Dad hands Sophia a grubby hanky and she blows her nose but goes on crying.

"It got out of hand – I said stuff and then we were doing it, and I didn't know how to tell you the truth and I almost began to believe it myself."

"Sorry?" I say, trying to listen to her through the noise in my head.

"I told you stuff, at the beginning, and I think

you wanted to believe it, so I told you more…"

I can't speak – someone's just pulled my world apart.

Sophia goes on. "That first night at the swimming pool, I suppose I thought you'd just ignore me, or say I was silly, but you didn't. So I kept going – I was sort of enjoying myself – and you were such a willing audience, it was easy, and yes, Ned's right, it was all wrong."

"You told me you didn't like him," I say, finding my voice. It sounds surprisingly calm. "That he isn't your dad. That he kept you apart. That you haven't heard from your mum for two months, haven't seen your mum in five years…"

Sophia's mum gives a cry. "Goodness – no! Five years? Five weeks, perhaps."

I pause, trying to make all the stories fit together. "You made out that he was an international criminal. You told me he was a murderer."

"Sophia?" says her mum, stroking Sophia's heavy black plait. "What have you told your friends?"

"I told them you were a singer."

"A singer? Well, I am."

"A princess."

"True also."

"And an actress…"

Sophia's mum smiles. "I am a singer — an opera singer."

"You didn't live in the flat with the cockroaches?" I ask.

"I once lived in a flat with cockroaches," says Dad, rearranging the sugar bowl. "Wonderful survivors."

Mum glares at him.

"No cockroaches," says Sophia, sounding defeated. "No flat in Maida Vale, no school with a checked dress, no rats."

"We have mostly lived in flats, that much is true," says Sophia's mum. "And it's true that since I married Trevor, I have seen less of Sophia. He felt it was better that she went away to school and as I travelled a great deal it made sense."

"Why didn't you come when we ran away?" says Sophia through her tears.

"Oh I did — I tried to — the police contacted me. I've been ringing Trevor twice a day, until he disappeared — goodness knows where he's gone — and I've been trying to get here. I emailed you, of course — I've been doing it every day. I can't tell you how difficult it is to get a flight to London from Christmas Island at this time of year."

"He's probably in Acapulco with all the other international criminals," says Ned.

"Shh, Ned," says Mum. "That's up to the police now. I'm sure they'll tell us when they find him."

Sophia's mum takes Sophia's hand and a little frown crosses her perfect brow. "I know Skyping and emailing twice a week isn't the same as being around much. I am sorry I have not been here to see you grow up – I am very sorry for that, my love."

"Skype?" I squeak. "I thought you weren't allowed near the internet?"

Sophia rubs her head against her mother's hand. "Sorry, Lottie."

They make the perfect mother and daughter picture.

Something boils up, something huge and purple and very, very angry. "Sorry? Sorry! Sorry for nearly killing us all, sorry for leading me across the country for nothing?" I slam my hands on the table-top, and a milk bottle jumps into the air and tips, flooding the table. I ignore it, I'm too furious. "I did it because I thought you were desperate, that there was no other way for you to see your mother! And then, and then it turns out that your mother's

here all the time – that she isn't dead or chained up or IGNORING YOU, she's here and she cares about you! And not only that – she emails you – you email her – you Skype – MORE THAN ONCE A WEEK. YOU ARE IN CONTACT WITH HER!" I step back from the dripping table. "I can't believe we went through with it – that you let me go through with it – you must be mad!"

"I wasn't mad – I was desperate – I haven't seen Mum for ages – months…"

"You're seeing her now!"

"But look what it took to see her. We've had to run away, wander around the countryside for days, eat out of bins…" Tears stream down Sophia's face.

"Oh darling…" says Sophia's mother. "Not eating out of bins? Surely not…"

I interrupt. "Not to mention the car crash and nearly being killed. Look what you did to me!"

"You didn't have to come."

"You told me you hadn't seen your mother for five years – of course I had to come."

"OK – that was wrong – but I couldn't think of any other way – and you seemed to want to come."

"I didn't want to be kidnapped – I didn't want

to be chained to a car leaking petrol into a ditch."

"Lottie! I didn't know that was going to happen and I certainly didn't plan it that way. I thought we'd find Mum, have lunch with her, stay in a hotel. I didn't think they'd kidnap us or that Wesson would nearly kill us, but please, see it from my point of view! You've got to understand, suppose you never got to see your mum – think about it." Her voice drops.

Mum and Sophia's mum are holding hands. They both look shocked. I'm shocked. Dad's rubbing his glasses, and Ned's drawing a smiley face in a pool of spilled sugar.

"Imagine running away time after time, hoping it would bring your mum, but it doesn't, it just brings a man in a suit with a bad temper. Put yourself in my place."

There's a choking noise from Sophia's mum and she reaches for Dad's filthy hankie.

"But you didn't tell me the truth! You could have told me the truth – there would have been other ways."

"I've tried everything else." Sophia's face is red and swollen; she no longer looks at all beautiful. "I couldn't get through to her any other way."

I can't even think how to answer her. A final surge of fury brings uncontrollable tears and I can't even see the table, Ned, Dad, Mum or Sophia.

I think I want to burst.

I think I want to explode.

Instead I go outside and stand in the rain.

An
understanding

What seems like hours later, Mum comes to find me. I've wandered out of the garden and into the fields. My trainers have wicked up all the water and I'm now more wet than dry, but I can't stop crying and until I do I don't want to go back into the house.

Buster came with me. He's soaking wet now, but he doesn't seem to mind.

"Ned was right," I mutter to Mum as she puts her arm around my shoulder. "He said it could be lies. But I wanted to believe it."

"I know, darling," says Mum. "I know."

"I wanted something exciting to happen," I say. "I get so bored, here — with just — plants."

Mum doesn't say anything, just turns me so that we're walking back towards the river.

"I know it sounds silly," I say. "But I wanted to be a hero."

She squeezes my shoulders. "It doesn't sound silly at all. I think we all want to be heroes. When I was your age I wanted to be a hero; sometimes, I still do. We all want to solve problems for other people — there's nothing wrong with it. Anyway, from what I heard, you *were* a hero."

"Was I?"

"You saved Sophia's life, and Miss Wesson's. If you hadn't broken out of that car you'd have all—" Mum stops. "It would have ended badly."

We walk a little further.

"But she told me she never saw her mum — at all, for years at a time, that he was stealing her mum's money, that he'd killed people, that he might even kill her mum. In fact, that her mum might already be dead."

"Yes," says Mum. "But imagine having someone coming between you and me, stopping us from seeing each other? She just wanted to see her mum."

I try to imagine it, and pull Mum a little closer.

"I suppose Sophia didn't tell you that her mum was Irene's niece," she says when we stop under a tree.

"What?"

"I thought I recognised her when she came in, so after you stomped out, I asked."

"Is that how Pinhead's been able to get hold of the house?"

Mum nods. "But because I asked, she now knows what he was up to, and she's going to find out how he managed to get the deeds. So there's still hope."

"Mum, do you think Pinhead's really a criminal?" I ask.

She laughs. "I don't know but he's not very nice, is he? That night in the kitchen I had him down as a bouncer."

"Snap!" I say, and laugh for the first time in ages.

"Do you want to go back in?" asks Mum.

But I don't. I'd rather stand in the wet.

So we wait to see Sophia climb into her mum's shiny little rental car and see it head off down the bumpy track, muddy water spraying up the sides.

Mum doesn't say anything, and we just wander back towards the house, kicking off our shoes in the damp porch, and padding into the kitchen, our wet socks making prints on the floor.

"She's gone," says Dad, unnecessarily.

I look up at Ned. I'm waiting for him to tell me he told me so but he doesn't. "Sorry, sis," he says. "Sorry we let it happen to us." He stands and comes over to me and puts his arms around my shoulders. It feels lovely.

"I've got something for you," I say, running for his bag that is sagging against the wall in the hall. I find Pinky and Perky and the mug with the sock and egg. "Here."

Ned picks it out and rolls the egg on to the table. "It's untouched. It even survived the car crash!"

I shrug, thinking of all the glass and mud and metal. "Miraculous," I say.

"Actually, it's not miraculous," says Ned. "It's to do with the design and makeup of the shell structure..."

"Shh, Ned," says Mum. "For now, it's miraculous."

I laugh, because I knew that's exactly what Ned would say.

Dad rustles around, rearranging scones on the

plate, while Mum refills the kettle and slams it on to the stove.

"I thought we were helping her," I say.

"I know, I know," says Dad. "No one'll blame you for what you did."

"Miss Sackbutt?" I ask.

Dad laughs. "Miss Sackbutt's just very relieved that you're back. She's not a woman to hold grudges. She's coming round later to see if you're all right."

"What about you and Mum?"

"Us?" says Dad. "It's been an interesting week, but we're just glad to see you home, safe."

"Really?" I ask.

"Really," says Dad, glancing at Mum, who is wiping her nose on her sleeve again.

When the rain stops Ned and I go for a walk together. I don't think we ever have before, ever, but there's a first time for everything. Dad gives us some money and we buy crisps and sweets from the post office, and although I've always thought we were missing out because we didn't spend our pocket money on crisps and sweets, they're a bit of a disappointment and what I really want is an apple.

"What did you think when you left me?" asks Ned.

I eat another spangle chew and think about it. "I think I thought I'd lost you for ever," I say.

"Really?" says Ned. "And how did that make you feel?"

He looks far too cheerful so I say, "Great, I felt great. It was such a disappointment when I saw you again."

Ned punches me on the arm.

It's fine – it's how it should be.

Miss Sackbutt turns up under a huge flowery umbrella.

"Lottie!" She drops the umbrella and wraps me in her arms before sniffing loudly and uttering, "Lottie," again. She smells of rose water and baked beans.

"I'm really sorry," I say, leaning her umbrella against the door. "I must have caused you the most enormous amount of trouble."

"No, Lottie – I'm the one who should be sorry," says Miss Sackbutt, sinking to a chair and fanning her face. "It's all my fault – I should never have trusted that Wesson woman. I can't even bear to think about it. And that man, he had such a lovely car, and nice manners." She raises her eyebrows so that they go outside her spectacle frames. "I'd no idea he wasn't what he seemed. I feel so silly."

Miss Sackbutt sits looking sad, somehow older and deflated as if someone popped her romantic bubble.

"I'm sorry for running away, though," I say, looking up at Mum who nods.

"Running away?" Miss Sackbutt's shoulders heave and she lets out a slow sigh, deflating still more. She gazes out of the kitchen door at the rain dripping from the ferns in the garden. "Running away's not a crime. Doesn't every child dream of running away? I know I did."

"Did you?" asks Dad, presenting her and Mum with cracked mugs of tea.

"Oh yes, several times," says Miss Sackbutt. "I once reached the Isle of Wight, you know." Miss Sackbutt examines a black spot on the side of the mug. "But I wanted to get to France. I wanted an adventure."

"How old were you?" I ask.

"Fifteen," says Miss Sackbutt, biting into a scone.

"I was in love."

Mum raises an eyebrow. "Who with?"

"Just France," says Miss Sackbutt. "I think I still am."

"Mum, what happened? I mean to you, and Dad and Ned."

I look up at Mum. She wipes the steam from the kitchen window as if she hasn't heard me. Eventually, she speaks. "The police found us very quickly the day after you'd left, and before Ned had returned. I was ready to throttle you. The story was very difficult to piece together. I couldn't believe you'd been kidnapped, and I couldn't believe you'd be stupid enough to follow a girl who has a repeated history of running away. I mean, you! Of all people. It was baffling – and very worrying."

"Sorry," I say.

"After a couple of days I felt that we'd entered a new kind of nightmare, where we lived in police stations and ate Pot Noodles."

"Oh."

"And then Ned came back to Bream in a police car, and of course I was massively relieved to see him, but it became more worrying still. I thought we'd have to search every scrap of the country, but in the end it was you that brought you back, you survived, you did all the right things. And I'm so glad."

Mum hugs me. I bury myself deep in her lumpy sweater and hug her back.

"And darling, why *did* you go with her?" asks Dad, as he's feeding Buster.

"Why?"

"Yes," says Mum. "You must have wanted something."

"I told you, I liked her story and I wanted an adventure – she offered one. And I made her a promise."

"Hmm..." says Dad.

"And," I say, my heart beating faster at what I might possibly be about to say. "And – I wanted to get away from all this..." I wave my arms to show the plants and tanks of scorpions. "It's not normal, you know – other people don't have all this – stuff."

Dad looks up and stares at me as if I'm talking Martian.

"Other people have parents in suits, and smart cars with dvd players."

"Ah," says Mum, looking at Dad. "We did wonder."

"It's just that we're not normal. I sort of wish we were normal – but then…"

I look around at the crumbling plaster, the dust, the piles of books, the chipped crockery.

"It's home."

Estonia

The phone rings. It's the police. They've found the flash drive. And they've found Pinhead. He's in Estonia.

"Sorry – the brake lines? So that would mean that all the brake fluid would leak out, wouldn't it?" Dad takes off his glasses and rubs his eyes as he listens to the person on the other end of the phone. There's a long pause. "Attempted murder – I see."

He listens again.

"I should think she's pretty furious."

More silence.

246

"So Maria Wesson would be a material witness then, she'd know exactly what he was up to?"

A pause.

"And what exactly *was* he up to?"

A pause.

"Sixteen million." Dad makes a long low whistle. "Oh my word! What a ridiculous amount."

A pause.

"Twenty-three companies in twelve countries? Why would anyone need so many?"

A pause.

"Squirrelling, was he? Robbing Peter to pay Paul. Of course, putting things in different pots all over the world, just in case."

A pause.

"So actually – yes, I understand. No – we won't tell a soul, not until it comes to court, but you'll have to extradite him, won't you? Hmm – could be a while then, but gosh, yes – lucky escape. Thank you. I will – yes, I will."

Dad puts down the phone and looks at me over his glasses. "You did well, Lottie sweetie. That flash thing had everything they needed on it and the woman, Maria thingummybob, spilled the beans on him. It seems he's been stowing Sophia's mother's money away for some time. Stealing from her and lots of other people, large amounts in dodgy European property deals. Sophia was right after all. Mr Pinehead is a very nasty piece of work. "

"And what about Wesson?" asks Ned.

"She was his lover and his accomplice, but his appearance in Estonia instead of Rio as they'd planned, and cutting the brake lines of the car she was driving, seem to have loosened her tongue. Can't help feeling a little sorry for the poor mug."

"Brake lines?"

Dad takes off his specs and rubs the lenses on his sweater. "It seems he tried to kill you all. He tampered with the car. She may have been driving badly, but she wouldn't have been able to slow down. He'd cut the brake lines; then once the fluid had leaked out she would have been unable to stop and the car would be lethal."

"Flip," says Ned.

"Oh," is all I can say.

Dad leans forward and pulls a hair from my face. "You really did do well, sweetheart."

"What about Irene's house?" asks Mum.

"They didn't say anything about that," says Dad.

"Perhaps he never actually got his hands on it."

"But he didn't kill anybody?" I ask.

"No," says Dad. "He didn't – so far as they know – but he tried. He tried to kill you. And he and his Estonian pals have stolen a great deal of money. So when they do catch him, he'll be going down for a long time."

We're playing UNO, now. All of us, in the house with the rain beating on the windows. It feels great, although something's still hanging in the air.

Mum's made pancakes. Dad's serving them up with mushrooms for supper. Ned laid the table, and we played cards while we waited. And it's lovely because we're all getting on together really well, but I can't help feeling that I ought to do something about Sophia. Trouble is, I don't know what.

The final
account

I don't actually do anything about Sophia for a week. I can't face her. Anyway, there's Ned's birthday to look forward to. It makes Mum and Dad tidy up for hours and hours beforehand; Dad even calls in a plumber who fixes the loo so that it doesn't sing every time it deigns to flush, and Mum moves the scorpions out into the greenhouse.

Encouraged by the comments of the plumber when he comes to call, Dad paints the hall and takes twenty-seven and-a-half pairs of leaky wellies to the dump along with a swampy paddling pool and a trampoline from Freecycle that never worked.

That drives Mum to get rid of her collection of *The Toxicology Month* magazines that she's been saving up since 1980 and clean out the cupboard under the stairs which leads to a man coming and wiping out the largest collection of woodworm ever seen.

They don't actually wear suits when Ned's friends turn up, but they do manage to look fairly ordinary, and Dad cooks frozen pizzas in the stove, even though he's always called them "money for old rope".

Ned's friends love the house, love the slugs, love the snails, love Mum's scorpions, love the fungi growing over the fridge.

Their parents actually sit on chairs and drink cups of tea when they come to pick them up, and Mum and Dad manage to talk quite normally.

No homemade champagne.

No dead chickens.

When I finally say I'd like to see Sophia, it's the day after Ned's birthday. Mum, Dad and Ned all hover in the background just in case I explode and kill her.

I'm not angry any more, just hurt. And puzzled.

She comes with her mum, who sits and drinks tea with my mum, like real mums do.

"What have you been doing since last weekend?" asks Sophia, keeping an arm's length between us.

I shrug. "Hanging out with Ned, appreciating him as my brother – helping mum with her scorpions, avoiding high places and cars."

Sophia laughs.

"What about you?"

"Getting to know my mum."

"Did she understand?" I ask.

Sophia stands and crosses the room. "She did – she apologised – I apologised. We watched TV together, cooked a meal, went for a walk."

"Why?" I ask, twisting my hair around my finger. "Why didn't you tell me the truth?"

She stares at the ceiling. It might provide an answer but I can't help feeling it should be coming from inside her head. "I thought you wouldn't get it – you wouldn't get that I just wanted to see my mum. And I wanted you to be my friend. You made me feel safe."

My jaw quivers as if I'm going to cry, but I don't know if they'll be tears of happiness or sadness. "Couldn't we have told the police, and then got on with being friends? Couldn't we just have hung out together – chatted, listened to

music, gone shopping — whatever it is other people do?"

"I didn't think it would work and, honestly, I didn't have you down as that sort of person. I thought you wanted a challenge. Sorry. I got it wrong."

"Actually, you didn't get it wrong. I'm not really a shopping sort of person — I mean — look..." I point at the crumbling plaster and the books crammed anyhow into the bookcase. "This is how I am, this is where I come from."

"Exactly," says Sophia. "That's why I like you."

"Like me? *Like* me? Then why did you do that to me?"

Sophia doesn't answer for a long time.

"I'm really sorry, Lottie. I'm really sorry for making you go through all that."

"Are you sorry for making me climb off that building?"

She nods her head.

"Sorry for making me eat from dustbins?"

She smiles.

"Sorry for nearly killing me in a car crash?"

She sucks in her breath and nods. I see tears in her eyes.

253

"And Sophia." I take a big breath. "I'm sorry for not understanding what it feels like to be separated from your family. I think I do now – or at least, I'm beginning to."

We step out into the garden. The sun's shining and Dad's mowed the grass. It almost looks like other people's gardens.

"We're moving to Irene's house," says Sophia.

"Oh?" I say.

"Mum and me. It belongs to her. She visited it when she was little and she loves it. She wants to repair it. She loves all of Irene's things, too. Mum showed it all to me and it's lovely, perfect as it is – well, without the trees in the gutters. What would you think of that?" she asks.

"Me?"

"Yes – you."

I think about it. Sophia living down the road. Sophia who likes an adventure. Sophia, the girl with whom I've had the best fun in my life.

"I'd think," I say, "that it was a good thing. A very good thing."